Happily Ever After

Published by: Al-Faatih Publishing UK

www.alfaatihpublishing.co.uk

Author: Maria Ahmed

Editing and Typeset: Al-Faatih

Cover: Mujib Abdur Rahman

ISBN: 978-0-9928729-2-2

Printed by Imak Ofset, Turkey

CONTENTS

Dedicated to every beautiful teenage girl.

May Allah protect you in this life and the next.

HANNAH

CHAPTER 1

Dear Diary: I dream of a land far, far away, where the sky is clear blue, the sand a bright yellow, and the cool ocean waves lap at my feet as I drink my juice under a palm tree, and some random people fan my face as I enjoy the silence – ALONE.

The sound of the crying baby really irritated me. Why did they have to bring her home? What was wrong with just us three in the house? Am I really that boring that they felt the need to have another child?

I slammed my diary shut and flopped on my bed face down. I hated them all! Since my parents told me that I was going to be a big sister, life really sucked. I was excited in the beginning, but reality soon dawned on me. I was expected to run around with my mum to buy new things for the 'baby'. I was no longer the baby, and instead I was expected to do a lot more around the house since my mum couldn't do much anymore - yes, she got bigger in size and was always tired! I had never even lifted a finger in the house before this! Housework was never my responsibility.

My dad started shouting at me over little things, and I couldn't even concentrate in school because I would be so tired from all the running around on the weekends. What was the point in having a new BABY!

I stuck my face into my pillow and growled really loudly. They had named her Aaliyah. She was only 5 weeks old but boy did she have an amazing set of lungs. She cried for hours... every hour... all hours. Why couldn't she just shut up and let me sleep at night sometimes?

I turned on my back to face the ceiling. I decided I needed a change. Maybe I should buy my own house and move out? Oh wait, I couldn't afford that just yet... What if I crashed at my friend Maryam's house for a while? I don't think her parents would like that... Maybe

I could sleep at one friend's house one day, and another friend's house another day... *that's just me acting homeless actually. All bad ideas. My brain feels fuzzy thinking.*

"Hannah! Hurry up and come downstairs, you have to go to the chemist for me remember!" I heard my mum shouting from the bottom of the stairs.

I got up and huffed my way downstairs, grabbed the money from my mum's purse and stomped out the door. In my thirteen years of existence, I never had to do so many jobs in my life. Now I felt wrinkly and old, even my hands looked like an eighty year olds from all the cleaning I had been doing. *Urgh.* I hid my hands in my pockets before someone saw them and called me 'Wrinkle Fingers'.

The boy at the chemist was from my school. He was doing work experience there because it was owned by his dad. *Fancy pants.* He gave me the tablets my mum needed on prescription, as well as some drops that Aaliyah needed.

"Erm, if you don't mind me asking..." he said in a quiet and almost nervous voice, "...are you okay? You look quite... angry."

He stared at me innocently, probably hiding a smirk that I knew was locked away somewhere. I knew more about him than he thought I did, and I didn't like him. It probably made his day to see someone as miserable and ugly as me. I looked straight at him.

"I *am* very angry, and it has nothing to do with *you, so don't bother trying to make it your business by asking me again!*"

Shocked by my aggressiveness, he tilted his head back. I kind of surprised myself at my harshness. *I was such a dude...*

I grabbed my things and walked straight - into - the - glass - door.
BANG.

Oh my god, oh my god, oh my god - *my face!* I felt dizzy, nauseous, and extremely embarrassed all at the same time.

"Oh no, are you okay!"

2

The pharmacist and the boy came running from behind the counter, unsure of whether I was going to collapse there and then, both of them running with their arms out as though I might just fall into their man-made net.

"I'm great thank you," I said, flapping my right hand up and down as proof that I was fine, holding my nose with my left hand, smiling freakishly. I opened the door and tried to walk out again, hopefully a little more lady-like, except this time with a red nose, red forehead, and I'm quite sure, a chipped tooth.

At home, no one even noticed (typical). Aaliyah was crying away, my mum was ssshhhhing and awwwwwing, my dad was blocking everything out by watching the news and really, I felt a bit lonely. I checked every millimetre of my teeth in the hallway mirror - no chipped tooth *alhamdulillah*. I rubbed my forehead and nose a few times to try and get their attention, but it obviously didn't work. So I decided to 'man-up' and picked up a book that a friend had given me. I think it was time I read and became an intellectual. It was about microbes and chemicals... *Right*.... So being intellectual wasn't for me.

I needed an adventure.

I texted Maryam asking her if she wanted to go to the park. She texted back straight away,

"Yes pls, c u thr in 10 mins."

I smiled. Maryam was probably being abused by her elder sister right now, that's why she seemed so eager to get out. Elder sisters were so evil... *The thought struck me...* Was I an evil sister too? I don't think I even knew what it was to be a 'good' sister because I'd been so busy running around... Or is running around exactly what a big sis does? I knew of so many girls who talked so happily about their little sisters - I wished I could do the same.

What's stopping me? Why do I act so moody at the sound of her name?

She's just a baby, silly Hannah, I told myself.

By the time I got to the park it was 2.30 p.m. I felt like swinging like a monkey from the monkey bars, so that's what I started to do.

"I totally hate her honestly, I wish she'd just disappear somewhere, or go and die in a corner..." Maryam started. "She's just such a WITCH! *Argh!*"

At that exact moment, Maryam fell off the bars and landed on the floor in a really un-ladylike manner. Well, that made the two of us.

"Hey, maybe that's a punishment for always hating on your sister!" laughed Saara as she walked toward us. Saara lived near us too - Maryam must have called her. We were like three Musketeers, joint by the hips, inseparable, or whatever.

"Shut up," said Maryam annoyed, wiping her clothes with her hands. "You really don't know what she's like. She offered to make me toast for breakfast this morning, and my mum, who thinks that Faria the Witch is actually nice, said, *'Aww see Maryam, isn't your sister sweet?'* Then mum went out to get something from the neighbours at no. 42, and Faria the Witch kept the bread in for so long that it came out of the toaster black as charcoal. She put it on a plate with ice cold beans, and said, *'Here you are sis, eat up'* with such an evil witch look on her face."

"You should have binned the toast and made some more," I offered as advice.

"It was the last two pieces of bread Hani," Maryam replied aggressively. "So I threw one at her face and went to my room. I've been in there since morning. Why do you think I came out here so fast?"

I laughed loudly, "We should get revenge on your sister... Let's tie her up to a lamppost and throw wet socks at her!"

"Oh my word, yeah. And then stick burnt toast to her head so she remembers what she did!" chirped Maryam. I knew creating fantasy stories about getting her sister back always cheered her up.

"Guys, sometimes you're too aggressive and take things the wrong way," Saara said while leaning against the railings. She never joined in when we would climb and swing like monkeys - how weird... *or were we weird...?* No, *she* was weird.

She carried on, "Sometimes, the best thing to do is to totally ignore the person who annoys you... they're only picking on you because they want to see your reaction... like Faria wants to see you all angry and worked up, so she keeps saying and doing things to you," she said, looking at Maryam.

Saara was like a wise owl sometimes. She really did have clever things to say... She was like one of them intellectuals I would like to be when I'm older. Except I think she was born an intellectual, because her mum said she was born talking sense. Her family seemed to love her a lot, and it looked like she loved them too. She had two younger brothers and one elder sister.

"True," said Maryam, now swinging gently from a swing. "I wish she would stop being so mean though. I really hate it. And I get angry so quickly, it's not *fair*. Why can't my mum see how horrible she really is?"

"It doesn't matter whether your mum sees how evil or good she is Maryam, it's about how good you make yourself," winked Saara.

"Well I'm annoyed at the new baby and how she cries *aaaall* night. I can't sleep. I feel like I'm the mum!" I said scowling.

Maryam laughed. "When are you going to stop calling her 'the new baby' and start calling her by her real name!"

"Aww I remember when my brothers were born, they would cry a lot too. You've just got to have patience Hannah, you'll learn to love her a lot soon. She can't talk - so she cries. That's her way of telling you that something's wrong. So look after her well. She's going to need you to hang out with when she's older." Saara looked keenly at me and then walked over and sat on the swing next to me.

I turned to look at her, "But why did my parents have her so many years later? I mean they could have had her a few years after me. But *thirteen years*! I don't understand why they'd do something like that."

Saara shrugged. "Maybe you should ask them Hani."

She was right. I leaned back and looked up into the whirling clouds. I felt like I had just been inspired.

I would certainly ask my parents why they had a baby thirteen years too late... or was it twelve years, considering she was inside my mum for nine months... no it was thirteen... This was confusing and I hated maths! Whatever it was – I needed to ask them the reasons for such a bizarre, life changing, Hannah-hating action!

Rain gently started to fall on our faces, so we stood up without saying anything to each other, and started walking. I liked that. I liked that we understood each other and could read each other's minds. I loved that we could walk without having to say anything, and be totally comfortable in one another's silence. I liked my two friends a lot.

"Guys, I'm going to go to the Mosque for my class, so I'll see you all tomorrow in school *inshaa Allah*," said Saara smiling.

"Mosque? Which one?" I asked. "I didn't even know you went."

"Yeah, Masjid Khaalid on Manor Lane. They've started doing a weekend class, I help out on Sundays. It's just teaching the kids about Islam. It's a lot of fun. If you're ever interested you should join me one day."

We nodded and she waved at us and gave us salaam.

"I think Saara is such a legend," said Maryam wrapping her cardigan around her tightly, "She's like the sister I wish I had in my house."

"I might take up her offer for next Sunday," I mumbled, hating in my head that I was going back home to the crying baby.

Oh man.

CHAPTER 2

The next week whirled by as quickly as the last.

I was stuck with English, Maths, Science and History homework throughout the week, and barely noticed the alarm clock going off in the mornings. It was finally Friday.

Wa-hey! I did a tap dance in my head, excited that the week was at its' end. I met up with Saara and Maryam outside our exceptionally cool meeting place – the red post box at the bottom of Clough Lane.

"What do you want to do after you finish school Saara?" I asked.

"Hmmm I'm still thinking," smiled Saara, almost secretly.

"And what are your thoughts to date?" I asked arching my eyebrow at her. That was a line my dad always used on me.

"Well, I could go down the medical route and be a doctor... but I'm not sure if I want to do that forever. Although it is really nice to be able to help people. Then I could go to different countries and help all the people there too. There's so much disease and poverty in the world," she said, deep in thought.

"Yeah but imagine all the sick things you're going to have to see!" squealed Maryam.

"But if it means helping others... we should be willing to risk everything for that. Isn't that what we're supposed to do as Muslims?" Saara was such a clever cat.

I nodded quietly, buried in my own thoughts. Saara was so good at helping others. She helped at the local Mosque and would donate in charity whenever she would hear that someone was raising money for something – anything – whether it was for the local library *(that needed demolishing in my opinion because it was so old)*, the elderly, children around the world, or for diseases like cancer. Muslim or not Muslim. She was so mature at such a young age *maasha Allah*.

I really wished I could be like her sometimes, or even break into her mind for five minutes and see how it worked.

Does Allah choose who will be intelligent, or do we make ourselves intelligent? Sometimes I feel so brain-dead and lazy, I can't figure out whether everyone feels like that, or if it's just me. I can't pretend that Allah made me like 'that', and so 'that's' the way I have to be... We all have the power to improve ourselves, so I should change myself, right...?

Maryam and I went into our Geography lesson, whilst Saara went off to have her quick meeting with our Head of Year, Mr Grayson. I had a feeling they were going to choose Saara to present at the next assembly! That would be *so* exciting! The last time she presented at the end-of-term assembly, parents had tears in their eyes. She had talked to everyone about our duties within society, and how we are role models for each other, despite our physical differences. There weren't that many Muslims in our area compared to other towns, but our school was a nice mix of different faiths and races.

We recently had some refugees from Albania joining us, and a Chinese family had moved into my street. In my year alone, there was a mix of English, Pakistani, Chinese, Indian, Bangladeshi, Irish, Moroccan, Somali, Burmese, German and Polish students. Multicultural week was always so amazing – because there would be so much to learn!

The best thing was that we all really got on, and there was very little to no racism in the school. I think it was because everyone treated everyone else like their equal – and would always help each other.

There was one racist P.E. teacher who started working at the school a few years ago. He would really pick on us girls who wore the hijaab and caused so many issues about us wearing it during P.E. My mum was one of the parents who went in to complain about him as well. *Go mother!* Anyway, for some reason or another he left (thankfully) and a much nicer teacher, Miss Andrews, replaced him.

As I entered class, my eyes immediately fell on Iqra Hosny Khan. *Oh no.* I really didn't want to see Cruella-de-Ville today, but lo and behold, there she was in the corner, with that big, ugly, slimy smirk plastered on her face. *My God, how I hated her.*

Just to fill you in, I have always had a hit-list in my head, of people I really dislike.. *Hate* is a strong word, so I prefer to call it 'dislike':

Iqra Hosny Khan aka Cruella-de-Ville

The Granny from No. 23

The Baby aka Aaliyah

The Boy at the Chemist

Khalid from the Takeaway

Sometimes the list shuffled about, in terms of priority, of who I hated the most. Like when Khalid would give me a burnt burger, he'd move up a few levels, and when Aaliyah would cry, she would move up. Granny from no. 23 really hated all children and would keep throwing things at us when we'd walk past. It was so strange.

Generally my list stayed the same though and Iqra was right at the top. She was a wicked, brutal excuse of a girl. She would walk past and accidentally kick you, or try and trip you, or flick things at you. She called me names like 'Bumba Head', just because I wore the hijaab. *Is that racism?* She's a Muslim too, so I never understood what her problem was. She once kicked the litter bin so it fell in front of me and I stepped right in the middle of it. *So embarrassing.*

And this was aaaaaall because I lived in the same area as her boyfriend, and our dad's were sort of friends. I don't even like boys! Guess who her boyfriend was? Punch-bag from the chemist. He wasn't nasty like her, but why did he have to talk to me, which then resulted in me getting abuse from his so-called other half. He was so stupid.

All boys are so stupid. Dating's haraam anyway, I don't talk to boys beyond our school work and studies. It's indecent. My parents have always told me to be careful because the Shaytaan is always around, and tricks you into thinking that you like someone, or they like you. And it isn't always true.

I pretended Cruella didn't exist and sat in my chair. Ms Flake came in, floated about the classroom telling us names of fancy countries and exotic destinations, and the lesson was over. It was then that Cruella came slithering over to me.

"So, Bumba, I heard you walked into a glass door last week?" She smiled like a Cheshire cat. Gosh she was so cruel.

"Actually, I was about to smack your boyfriend because I couldn't find you that morning, and obviously I felt sorry for him because he isn't quite as cruel and weird as you, so I smacked the door instead... with my head," I replied, as cool as a cucumber, and walked off.

Take two! I giggled to myself. Oh how I loved walking away with my head held high from this dumb couple! This time (fortunately) I didn't walk into any doors.

I heard some girls laughing behind me, obviously at Cruella, but I didn't look back. Maryam came jogging behind me, giggling away.

"Oh my God I *cannot* believe you just did that! Her jaw dropped to the ground! High-five sister!"

I turned to face Maryam and high-fived her hand with my wrinkly, eighty year old hand. We met up with Saara for lunch and Maryam told her all about my big act. Apparently everyone in our year was now talking about it. Big deal. I wasn't even bothered, I just wanted Cruella off my back.

Saara told us that she was definitely going to be presenting the end-of-term assembly once more. We congratulated her and I felt so proud of her! She was so shy and sheepish generally, but once she started talking, it was as if she would drown out everyone else who was there, and just focus on talking to each and every person in front of her. You never felt 'left out' with Saara.

"What do you think my topic should be?" she asked.

"Hmmm, let's see. How about importance of education?" said Maryam whilst finishing off her pizza slice.

"Or manners and importance of family life?" I offered, swirling my pasta round and round in a mix up of three different sauces.

"Hah! Funny that you would think family life is important, considering you hate your little sister and all that," smirked Maryam.

"Whatever! You're no better, with your hatred for your elder sister!" I snapped back.

Inside however, I knew that what she had said was true. I knew family life was very important. Your parents, brothers, sisters, uncles, aunties, grandparents - they're all part of the happy society we live in. I couldn't imagine life without all these lovely people around me. Why then couldn't I just begin liking Aaliyah and be happy about her being around?

Just as we finished our lunch and put our trays away, my form teacher, Mrs Hayes, came looking for me.

"Hannah, could I see you in my office please?" she said in her usual, bored, half asleep manner from the cafeteria doors.

My heart hit the ground, was this because of what I said to Iqra? Surely it wasn't offensive was it? Would they kick me out of school for this? Would I have to move to another school! Oh no! My mind went into over-drive and I started thinking of every possible scenario about to unfold.

Saara and Maryam just stared silently as I followed her, grabbing my things. Maryam still had her spoon of yoghurt half way to her mouth - her mouth still open.

"Oops," I heard her say to Saara as I walked through the cafeteria.

My dad was standing waiting for me in the office looking tired, red-eyed, almost like he had been... crying (*what?!*). Surely this couldn't be that big of a deal... *could it?* I stood next to him, without saying a word, silently cursing that Cruella for whatever story she might have made up.

As if she had read my mind, Mrs Hayes said, "Don't worry Hannah, you are not in trouble dear, your father's come to take you home due to an emergency."

"Oh," I said, looking up at my dad, who still hadn't said a word. He smiled half-heartedly to Mrs Hayes, said thank you, and started walking out.

11

"Come on Hannah," he said, way too quietly.

I held his arm. "What's wrong dad?"

He gave me a slight hug and let his arm hang on my shoulder. He still hadn't smiled at me.

Once we got out of the building and were in front of the car, he stopped.

"Hannah," he turned to face me. "Your sister, Aaliyah... she isn't well. She's sick. She's in hospital... We need to go and see her."

He opened the front door of his Audi for me, and then went around to the driver's side and got in.

"What do you mean, 'she's sick'? What's wrong with her?" I was confused.

He started the engine. "She's got an illness. Cystic Fibrosis."

My mouth fell open and then my heart hit the ground. My baby sister was sick with Cystic Fibrosis. I had never known anyone who had it, and I didn't even know what it was really. But I knew it was serious because I had learnt a little about it in school.

Why did she have it? How? I didn't understand anything. Was she born with it? What caused it? And how come he needed to come and get me from school? I wanted the answers but I also knew I shouldn't keep asking my dad at that point. I knew it would be better for me to wait until we got to the hospital. My poor dad - he looked so distraught. He really must have been crying before he came to get me.

We drove in complete silence for the next twenty five minutes.

CHAPTER 3

We arrived home late in the evening.

The hospital visit had been depressing. My mum looked as bad as my dad had, with red eyes, and a seriously upset face. I wanted to cry as soon as I saw her. Aaliyah was hooked up to all this machinery and nurses and doctors were in and out doing tests and throwing medical terms to each other. It was just chaotic.

The baby hadn't cried at all though, weirdly. I had asked mum and dad how long they had known, and my mum said it was from this morning after I had gone to school. She took Aaliyah to the GP and he had referred her to the hospital immediately.

I hated myself. I hated that I had hated the baby who cried all night. I hated that I had hated the baby who cried all night because she was sick... seriously sick. I felt panicked.

I got up to reach for the tasbeeh my mum kept in the living room, and started doing istighfaar (asking Allah's forgiveness), looking at each bead as I said the word "astaghfirullah" carefully and slowly before passing the bead on. I was doing this because I didn't know what else to do, and I felt empty inside.

Once, Saara had told Maryam and I that doing istighfaar was a really soothing yet important thing to do at least once a day.

"It helps me unwind, and at the same time I get rid of all the sins I've committed in the day..." I remembered her words... word for word.

My mum was staying in the hospital overnight, and the house was deadly silent. I finished the tasbeeh and wrapped it around my wrist as a good will sort of thing, in case I needed to do it again - I don't really know why it felt good to do that. I made my way to the front room where I knew my dad was sitting. I quietly opened the door and thankfully it didn't creak as it normally did, with its dodgy hinges.

My dad was sitting on the sofa, totally still, his head leaning back, eyes closed, hands raised in front of him in du'aa, murmuring to himself. If I didn't know the situation and the agony he was in right now, emotionally, I would have thought he'd gone mad. I felt the blood drain from my face as I heard him sobbing quietly, repeating the same two lines,

"Why O Allah, why? Relieve us of this distress O Allah, relieve us of this distress..."

I watched him and tears formed in my eyes. This baby - who was incapable of speaking, or wiping her own bottom, or eating by herself - had already developed such a strong bond with my father. It was as though his whole world had collapsed just by her being labelled with an illness. Was it that serious? I didn't dare ask my parents what exactly was going on in the hospital, because I had a feeling my mum would literally burst into tears again. She was exhausted from crying so much, it seemed. I ended up crying too, I don't know why, or how, or what forced me.

I thought I hated the kid? I didn't realise how much I actually cared about the little doll of a baby sister I had, until I saw her lying there asleep, abnormally silent, breathing through a tube. My mum didn't take her eyes off her the whole time I was there, and had held my hand tightly as if for comfort or support. I just sat next to my mum, watching her and the baby, protectively gripping the hand of the woman who had given birth to me and raised me the best she could. My dad was sitting on a chair on the other side of the cot trying so hard not to cry.

I had really never seen any of them like that - especially not my dad. Women cry all the time, and cry even when they're happy for some reason, but men are so good at hiding their emotions. It hit me, that until today, *I had never seen my dad cry.* Did my parents care this much about me when I was a baby? Would this have happened to them if I was ill? *Obviously you idiot,* I scolded myself, *stop thinking about yourself all the time!*

I needed to do some research into this mysterious illness. I left the door slightly open so as not to let my father know that I had been stood there, dragged myself into the living room and fired up his Mac laptop.

"What is Cystic Fibrosis?"

CHAPTER 4

" ...And so gravity, as we already know, was discovered by Newton..."

Mrs Smith droned on. She was so boring. And so draining. And so... so... slow at talking.

Normally I would have been sneaking funny notes to Lisa who sits on the table next to mine. Mrs Smith never noticed and we had been doing it for three years *successfully*. I wasn't in the mood though. I hadn't been in the mood all weekend.

I had been in and out of hospital with dad. Mum was still staying at the hospital with Aaliyah.

Aaliyah... my poor baby sister.

I wondered what life would be like when she was my age, thirteen. I would be twenty six. Probably married, probably with a wrinkly face, and hopefully with a good education and life. But every time I thought of Aaliyah reaching thirteen - I shivered inside. Would she have a happy childhood? Or would it be one where she's in and out of hospitals every week, to help cure her? Oh Lord, *will she even survive to thirteen?* I had been reading up about Cystic Fibrosis all weekend. It isn't abnormal for sufferers of Cystic Fibrosis to live for months to years, depending on how serious it is. I didn't know the extent of Aaliyah's... I was bound to be thinking the worst.

I wondered how dad was getting on at work today... He was still as upset this morning as he had been since Friday when he picked me up. We had barely spoken to each other. Normally I rambled on and on, but I didn't feel like it... for the first time in my life.

Saara, Maryam and I met up at the school gates at 3.20 p.m. after Maths. I was in Set Two for Maths, and Maryam and Saara in Set One. I hated Maths. Every living cell in my body, every bone fragment, every ligament, every nerve, all cried out *"We hate Maths!"* every morning.

I carried my bag home like it was a dead body. It felt so heavy on Mondays.

"Why do teachers give us so much homework on Mondays? You'd think they'd give it on Friday," I complained.

"It's all a part of the evil-teachers-plan," Maryam snapped. "I was in trouble today by Mr Raheem for dropping my ruler in class."

Saara laughed out loud, "That was because it fell three times! He thought you did it on purpose!"

"I didn't though! It's not my fault the stupid thing kept jumping to its' death," snarled Maryam. "I've got a detention because of it!"

Oh boy was she angry.

"Well, maybe your ruler kept jumping because your bag stinks really badly, give it a wash," I smiled, and then burst into laughter at my own joke... I hadn't laughed in three days, and it felt good.

"Shut up Boomerang Feet."

I laughed at that too. Maryam had called me 'Boomerang Feet' since I won her in a race in the first week of Year 7. That's actually how we met. She called me Boomerang Feet, I called her Flat Feet, and told her to get her feet checked by the Doctor because they were abnormal. We became close after that. Odd way to make a friend...

"When's your detention?" asked Saara trying to keep the smirk out of her voice after mine and Maryam's not-so-polite comments to each other.

"Wednesday," replied Maryam, ever-so-*flatly*.

I got home to an empty house. It was weird mum not being here. Dad had left a note for me on the table with instructions on what to eat, and how to make it for myself. Then there was another sticky note saying,

"Lock the front and back doors, and don't open any windows or doors for any strangers. I've got my key. Stay at home, and don't go out for anything. Please."

I smiled to myself. Dad was so sweet and I loved him to bits. It was 3.45 p.m. and he would be back at 5 p.m. - which meant I had one hour and fifteen minutes of boredom. I had never had to experience being home alone before. Considering that I don't consider myself 'normal' for various reasons, I wondered what *normal* people do when they're home alone? I went upstairs to get out of my drab uniform and have a quick shower. I was back down by 4 p.m., and I put the food in the microwave and sat down on the dining chair waiting for the fifteen cooking minutes to be over.

I ate, in silence. The silence was really getting to me, it was really, really, *really* weird not having Aaliyah crying in the background. I had to admit, I was really missing it. I couldn't wait to see her later *insha Allah.*

Dad got home at 5 p.m. and we left straight away. As we entered the main doors of the Children's Hospital, I saw a kid in a wheelchair in front of me, two kids crying so hard that they couldn't breathe to my left, and paramedics rushing a kid in from behind us as everyone stumbled out of their way.

Wow. This was life. This was reality.

All day long children are rushed in through these doors for one emergency or another. Whatever the emergency is, it may not seem serious to other people, or as serious as another person's, but it is serious. And it is scary. And it totally breaks you to pieces if it's your family, or your brother and sister who is in a life-threatening situation. Ask me, I've experienced it.

I felt like a ghost watching the many scenes unfold in front of me. My dad had stopped also, probably noticing that I wasn't following him anymore, and was looking at me from the escalator.

"Hannah, are you okay?" he asked.

I looked up at him, snapping out of my daze. "Yeah dad, sorry." I caught up to him.

We went up in the escalator to the seventh floor where Aaliyah's temporary home was, the Reindeer Ward. I felt a rush of excitement knowing I would get to see her again.

CHAPTER 5

On Wednesday, Maryam had her dreaded detention, and so for the first time in absolute ages, Saara and I walked home together without her.

I poured my heart out to her about Aaliyah on the way back. I was feeling more upset than usual. She listened and was a caring friend as always, giving good advice about how everything good and bad is from Allah, and we aren't capable of changing anything if it's meant to be - so we shouldn't worry.

After school it was the same routine of me eating at home alone, dad coming at 5 p.m., and going to the hospital. After we went in, mum got up to go for a walk since she had been in Aaliyah's room all night and all afternoon - and that must seriously have felt like being in *prison*. Hospitals are so depressing. I offered to go with her and on the way tried talking to her, but I knew she wasn't really in the mood, so I stopped twittering on.

When we got back to the room, the regular nurse was sitting and talking to my dad. He was really nice, and Aaliyah was under his care most days. He was a Muslim, quite young, and really got on with my dad. I silently thanked Allah for giving my dad someone he could talk to - he hadn't met or spoken to any of his friends since Aaliyah had gone into hospital. Plus, the nurse genuinely cared about us all, especially my mum.

"Oh mum, you forgot to get yourself some tea!" I suddenly remembered.

"Don't worry Hani, Idrees got me some just an hour ago," she smiled at him as she said this, and he got up from the chair noticing that we were now in the room.

"Aunty, are you talking about me again!" he laughed. "Hey Hannah, hope you're doing good today. Aaliyah's looking much better," he chirped. He had just given Aaliyah some medicine and began picking the things up to leave.

"Idrees, don't forget to come by this evening to collect the key okay?" My dad gestured to him and then sat back down as he nodded and walked out.

We got home late that evening and I went straight into my room. I had homework to do but I didn't have the energy. I listened to the silence. The house was no longer alive with the crying of Aaliyah. It was dead. And it was boring. And I hated it. I wished she would come back.

Tears welled in my eyes. I remembered what Saara said to me after school today,

"When you feel upset, go down in prostration, and ask Allah for whatever you want to ask of Him. Your forehead is on the ground, but your words will reach the Heavens. Be sincere, beg Allah. He wants you to ask. He can make anything happen."

I quickly picked up the prayer mat in my room, the one that my Aunty bought me from 'Umrah, and rolled it out. I dropped to my knees and facing the Qiblah, threw my head in my hands and cried, and cried, and cried. I couldn't help it.

O Allah, bring her back home! I promise I'll never complain again! I promise I'll help my mum with everything I possibly can, and do more than I've ever done before!

I felt mixed feelings inside me - was I more concerned about my sister, who I barely knew, or was I more concerned about the pain my mum and dad were clearly feeling? Was I concerned because I knew I had been selfish all this time and had paid little to no attention to the problems of my small family? I knew it was a mix of all those things.

I didn't bother asking much about Aaliyah when she was born, because I didn't appreciate her. Did my parents notice how weird I became when she was born? *O Allah, did that upset them even more! Have they cried because of me!*

Suddenly, realisation hit me hard. We learnt it in Biology today. The answer to my big question, *'Why did my parents have Aaliyah thirteen years later?'* Miss Archwell told us, and I was barely paying attention. She explained how sometimes couples can't have children at all, and have to undergo medical treatment to try and have children. They might have a child after so many years. Or, in other cases, a couple may have a child, but then develop a medical problem and that stops them from being able to have any more. Sometimes they then have kids, *years later*, other times, they just never do. *O Allah...*

Tears of anger and hatred for myself rolled down my cheeks. I went down into sajdah. This is the one place I can connect with Allah, and it feels like there is no barrier between me and Him. It's just me, and my Creator. Just me, and my Best Friend. I don't even have to say anything, and He understands me.

This was one of them times.

Inside, I realised how selfish I had been - how horrible and how bitter - to say things to my sister because I saw my parents cuddling and molly-coddling her, when really, my parents were ecstatic because they had *finally* had another child. To me, it meant an enemy. To them, it meant a bigger and a happier family. And I had ruined it, with my bitterness, my jealousy, and my greed of my parents love. Had Aaliyah become ill because of my swearing at her under my breath every day?

Is it really that important for me to think that my parents can only love me? Don't they have enough love to share with everyone else? In 'normal' families where there are lots of children, they always complain that their parents don't love them enough, or love the other brother or sister more, but really, is it such a bad thing? What's the big deal? If today my parents show me more love, and I feel happy inside, tomorrow they can show Aaliyah more love, and that's fine, because that's fair. I shouldn't complain.

O Allah! I promise I will not complain! O Allah, you know exactly how I feel, and I can't even put it into words, please just cure Aaliyah and bring her home to me!
I will look after her, feed her, and even change her nappy!

I sobbed continuously in sajdah, in front of my Allah, for what seemed like an eternity. I didn't open my eyes once, and I didn't move at all. I promised myself again and again, *things will be different from now on.* I felt that I hadn't done enough for my parents. All the nappies they had changed of mine, all the nights I had kept them awake, and now Aaliyah - all of them favours needed to be repaid back. I needed to give them happiness the way they had tried to give it to me all my life, *even though I never understood it most of the time.*

Eventually I got tired and my tears dried out. I gently lay on my right-hand side, my face wet, my eyes probably redder than ever. My throat felt hot. I had never cried like this before.

At some point, I fell asleep.

CHAPTER 6

I woke up suddenly.

I was still lying on the floor in my clothes, on the prayer mat - in a muddle. I looked at the clock on my wall - 06:00. It was still dark outside. I had been here all night, *wow*. I felt as stiff as a log, so I got up to stretch and to go to the bathroom.

I opened the door quietly and saw a faint light from under my parent's room. *Dad was awake?* I used the bathroom, and felt a sudden urge to do my wudhoo' as well. I was sure it was Fajr time because it was still dark outside. I normally do wudhoo' in the mornings - it's a habit my mum had trained me to do from the start and made sure I always did. But salaah was a habit I needed to sort out – I rarely prayed my Fajr.

I'd normally wake up last minute for school and spend the little time I had on doing what was important for me - like scrubbing the night-grime off my face with a good facial wash, brushing each tooth individually for maximum whiteness, making sure my face looked good with facial creams and very light makeup, quick breakfast, and then spending the last bit of time on my hijaab. If I had less time, I'd sacrifice my breakfast time, for my hijaab time. It had to be done. Sometimes I would miss my salaah during the day, especially when I was at school. But today felt *different.*

I did my wudhoo' and left the bathroom happy. I felt revitalised all of a sudden. As I was going back to my room my dad poked his head round from his bedroom door.

"Hannah?" he asked, clearly surprised.

"I woke up and needed the bathroom... So I thought I'd pray my Fajr as well."

My dad suddenly smiled a huge smile. "Really? *Maasha Allah* Hannah... I'm surprised. You're a good girl."

I smiled back at him and it hit me that this was the first time he had smiled in so many days.

Was me praying salaah a source of that much happiness for my dad?

I made an intention to read my Fajr tomorrow as well. I prayed and went downstairs to the living room. I had until 8.30 a.m. before I had to leave for school.

I saw the TV staring at me. I felt a sudden twitch to put it on as I normally would when I'm bored. Yet at the same time I was overwhelmed with this unexplainable feeling, that I shouldn't waste my time watching it.

Life is too short to do meaningless things, I thought. My fingers stopped twitching for the remote, and I just stared at the television. It hit me that the big black box hadn't been turned on for so many days, and no one even cared. What a waste of time it really was. I certainly wasn't going to watch it. *Things would now be different.*

I still had my hijaab on from Fajr, so I decided to pray some Qur'aan. It felt as if I hadn't read it in such a long time. I sat on the floor in front of the fireplace and began to recite quietly.

My dad walked in at about 7.30 a.m. ready for work. I looked up at him and he smiled at me - that same big genuine smile he gave me earlier.

"I see Hannah is re-connecting with the Qur'aan?"

"Yes dad. After seeing you read it every day, I know I need to get into a habit too." I smiled back.

"Have you finished? Let's have breakfast," said Dad.

As I put the Qur'aan away he got our bowls and cereal boxes out.

"You know Hannah, Aaliyah being ill is very difficult for us all right now, especially your mum. I keep telling her that it's a test from Allah, and we need to remind ourselves about this all the time, but she's still very upset - naturally. Everything good or bad that happens is from Allah. We shouldn't complain. Maybe you should take something for your mum to try and cheer her up. We'll stop in at a shop on the way to the hospital later. It'll make her day."

Wow, my dad was talking to me like a grown-up. This was a first!

"Yeah dad... I agree. Mum looks so... torn. I really hope Aaliyah gets better soon... *insha Allah.*"

"Don't we all Hannah," dad said to himself quietly.

We sat to eat our breakfast in silence. Today was a new day. I could feel it inside me. I was beginning to understand the world better. I was beginning to understand that when you're young, everything seems unfair and cruel, yet at the same time everything appears so simple. In reality, it isn't.

Our parents go through things that are unimaginable, but they stay happy and keep smiles on their faces – we teenagers just can't see the trouble they go through. It's as though they feel they need to protect us, so they don't tell us the details of their problems.

Tomorrow, it will be us in that situation.

I wondered how well I would deal with having a child in my arms who could die at any point.

CHAPTER 7

My spirits were somewhat lifted in school over the next few days.

I was more composed, and began paying attention in class again. When I thought of Aaliyah, I had this huge hope inside me that Allah would bring her back home safe, and if she was going to be ill for the rest of her life, I would look after her with all my heart, and never let her feel pain or discomfort again.

And if, for whatever reason Allah knew best, she didn't come back home - I knew I would look after my mum and dad like never before. I was committed, and I would do whatever they told me to do, whether I liked it or not, just because I never, ever, wanted to see them this upset again.

I was becoming a stronger person.

I even managed to talk to Cruella with a smile when we were forced to partner up for problem solving in Maths. Of course she wasn't happy about it, well, neither was I really. But I got on with it, which was different for me. Normally I'd complain first and pull a face, and then make it obvious I hate her, and then do the work. This time the process was a lot easier. I just got on with it. Things really were feeling different.

Maybe this was all the barakah (blessing) of praying my Fajr and reciting Qur'aan in the morning?

Maryam was busy in the library during the short break period on Thursday, and as much as I loved her, I felt I needed some one-to-one time with Saara, which again, was something new as the three of us had no secrets. Yet I felt that only Saara would understand me in what I was feeling.

"Saara, do you ever feel that you've poured your heart out so much, and cried to the point that you now feel you can't cry anymore because there's nothing left inside, so instead, you start filling your heart up with love, happiness, good feelings - positivity even?"

I asked her, searching her face for an indication that she understood what I meant. Saara looked up at me, seeming a little surprised at what I had said, and then smiled. I sat down on the chair next to her in the canteen.

"Yeah, I actually do." She smiled again. "Why, are you feeling different or something?"

I looked up at her thinking of how I could explain my feelings to her.

"I really am. I don't know what's happened to me. It's like all of a sudden I've started doing things that I wouldn't normally do. It's only been a few days but I had this breakdown once - following your advice actually. I prayed to Allah and literally just felt like I was pouring my heart out to Him. Within a day or two that was it. It's as if I've grown overnight, not in size but I mean inside me. My brain maybe? I don't know! I suddenly feel stronger, more sensible, more understanding of the world, of my place in this world? I mean I've even started praying my Fajr every morning, I make my dad his breakfast every morning, I've been going to the hospital and tidying up the room, getting my parents drinks. I mean it's no big deal right, but normally, I'd just sit there and they would do everything for me. So it's weird. I've even started smiling at people I don't know!"

I threw my hands up in the air with my last comment. It must have been the icing on the cake, because Saara had been listening and watching me intently and seriously, and then started laughing at that.

"Smiling is a sunnah of our beloved Prophet isn't it Hani, so that's actually a brilliant thing," she said. "It seems like you've just suddenly matured. I mean puberty isn't just the physical changes, but it's also the emotional and psychological changes. You understand more, and you understand better. Little things become important to you, things you wouldn't have paid attention to before - like you said - you've now started caring for your parents more, and before that you would never have thought of doing it. When you mature, you listen more than you talk. That's really important. A lot of teenagers don't do that, and that's a big mistake."

She paused for a few seconds, and her face became serious and thoughtful.

She carried on, "I'm actually amazed at all this you know Hannah. If you think about it, Allah put you through a test and difficulty, and from it, you've gained happiness. I mean, Aaliyah became ill and seriously sick, and that's what has made you come closer to Allah. And you smiling, being happier inside, having a positive mind – that can only be when you're close to Allah. So obviously, *maasha Allah*, you are close to Allah right now. You're praying Fajr, you're taking care of your parents, you've got good intentions on how to treat everyone - including Iqra who you can't stand! You're doing everything right. That's why you're feeling content and peaceful inside - because Allah loves you. Most teenagers, or adults even, don't have that. Even the mature ones. But this is what Allah has told us, that sometimes a thing will happen to us, and we think it's bad, but actually it's really good.

Aaliyah became ill, which is very sad for us all, but it's brought you and your family closer together, you've become a better person. If she hadn't gotten ill, would you love her and your parents as much as you do right now? Probably not."

My eyes lit up. What an observation. Everything she had said was true.

"And Allah also says that sometimes a thing will happen to us, and we think its good, and we really want it, but actually it's really bad for us. Like, I don't know, say with having a boyfriend or listening to music or watching TV or something. None of them things are good for us, but we want them and we think we need them. Or a better example, is if someone suddenly gained lots of money, and we all thought, wow she's so rich with so much money, but really, that money could kill us if we had it. I mean loads of rich people are depressed or commit suicide.

So things are not always what they seem. In your case, you seem to have passed this huge test, and you've become a friend of Allah just by praying to Him. See what prayer and sajdah and crying and talking to Allah can do Hani? If everyone did that, it would solve the world's problems, I promise you."

"Does it happen to you often?" I asked, "I mean do you feel the need to talk to Allah a lot?"

"Yeah, I do. All the time. Every night. Sometimes during the day when I'm just sitting there as well. He knows what you're feeling all the time doesn't He. You don't even have to say anything sometimes."

"I know I've never asked you this before and it sounds really weird but... do you cry when you're doing du'aa?"

She paused for a few seconds, and her face dropped a little. I was watching her every expression for some unexplainable reason. It was as if her expression and opinion mattered to me more than anything else in the world at that point. Well, I guess it did because after all, she was the wisest thirteen year old girl I knew. Seriously, you'd have to meet her to understand what I mean if you hadn't clicked on already. She experienced things that normal girls hadn't. She would think of things that normal thirteen year old girls wouldn't. She was just... *different.*

"Yeah, I guess so."

"Why though Saara? I mean I've been crying because of my baby sister having the probability of dying any time if she doesn't get better, and seeing my parents so upset all the time and teary eyed. It drives me insane. But you? *Maasha Allah* you've got a lovely happy family, you're always so nice to each other, I can't imagine what would upset you?"

There was a long pause. She kept her eyes down.

"I guess Hannah there are things that everyone feels, you can't always explain them, but whether you're happy or sad, you need to talk and cry to Allah. Sometimes there may be a reason, sometimes there may not be. But you need to talk to Him to feel better. One person might have a problem that seems more than another person's because they talk about it a lot, or you find out about it, but really, the second person has problems as well - ones that they don't show, but are always in their mind."

She smiled a way too brief and quick smile and stood up, indicating the end of our conversation. I wanted to get to the bottom of Saara's problems, and the thought hit me -

she had never complained about any problems... *ever.* Then why did she look so sad? At the same time, I could tell she didn't want to talk about them right now, whatever they were, and that was just fine with me - I wouldn't push her because she was too special to me. I linked my arm into hers and we walked down to our next class.

I felt better already. Saara was an inspiration for me in my life *maasha Allah.*

CHAPTER 8

I got home after school on Friday with a seriously bright idea - I would cook for my dad!

Well... when I say 'cook' I mean... microwave or grill cook. I took some food out of the freezer, and put the grill on. I've always wanted to learn how to cook, I think it's really cool being able to suddenly make something, or to have a midnight feast that you've quickly made. Obviously you can only eat such a feast if you know how to make it... I made a plan in my head that *insha Allah* when mum and Aaliyah came home, I would learn. I had watched and helped my mum sometimes, I think I was just lazy though. *Things will be different.*

Dad was amazed at what I had put together for him when he got back from work. He had a twinkle in his eyes that I hadn't seen in weeks. He ate quickly, thanked me for the food, kissed me on the forehead, and got ready as I cleared the dishes and got ready for the hospital super-fast.

I was excited to see Aaliyah and mum as always, and the best thing was that Aaliyah seemed to be recovering. It was another prayer come true when we went in today though. A senior consultant was checking Aaliyah as we entered the room. My parents had been looking forward to this day all week − what he would tell them today was going to matter.

I told my dad he could go in while I went back and waited outside. I knew it was going to be serious talk, and my mum and dad would get really upset if it was bad news. It just didn't feel right to be inside at that time. Plus, there didn't seem to be much space inside the tiny room with all the nurses and doctors in and out of it. I was sitting outside for about half an hour before the door opened and the entourage of doctors and nurses left with the senior consultant at their lead.

As they left, the tall greying consultant man turned back and smiled at me. I shyly smiled back and nervously got up to go inside, wondering what had been said, my heart beating at a hundred miles an hour. Was Aaliyah okay?

I was almost shaking as I opened the door and peeped in.

My dad had his arm around my mum and was looking down at Aaliyah's cot. I couldn't see his face clearly because he was turned to the side. My mum had her face covered with her hands. As I walked in, she moved her hands and walked as fast as she could to me with tears running down her face. I was terrified. She bent down and grabbed me, hugging me as tightly as she could.

"Hani!" she sobbed. "She's okay, everything's going to be okay, she can go home!"

Wow.

I was stunned into silence. Aaliyah was going to be okay? I realised at that point, these weren't tears of upset or pain on my mum's face - these were tears of joy. My dad also turned around and smiled at me, with such a huge, relieved smile, that I knew that whatever had been said in the last half hour or so, was brilliant news. I hugged my mum tightly and held on to her hand as we walked over to Aaliyah's cot. There were no wires covering her and no machinery around her. She was in a simple yellow baby-grow, and a cream coloured blanket was over her. She looked absolutely adorable *maasha Allah*.

My dad hugged me as I stood next to him and I hugged him back, still tightly holding my mum's hand. It was like a perfect family portrait - all three of us looking down on this troublesome baby who had moved us to tears every single day of her short life. But we loved her so very much. I loved her now more than I had ever loved her before. She was my baby sister.

Idrees the nurse popped his head round the door. "I'll have the discharge letter ready ASAP uncle. Many congratulations to you all," he said with a huge smile.

I said *alhamdulillah* a hundred times automatically in my head. Allah was *so* Merciful, and He had answered our prayers. I didn't care to ask anything at all about what the consultant had said, because I knew what the conclusion of the story was:

We were going home *insha Allah.*

MARYAM

Chapter 1

Dear Diary: I seriously hate her guts. When is she going to get LOST out of my life?

This is the basic thought that runs through my head every morning when I see my sister. You know how you meet people and you be yourself – nice and normal – and then suddenly without warning they attack you or say something nasty about you, or embarrass you – and you did nothing to instigate their rudeness. So you stay quiet and let it pass.

"She must be having a bad day," you think to yourself. But then, some time later, you're being your nice and normal, happy self again, and voila, there she goes again with the insults. And again. And again. And *again.*

Well that's the relationship me and my sister have. And before you think anything negative about me, hey – I'm only human, I can only take so many beatings before I start to fight back!

No word of a lie, she winds me up. Every day. Every hour. Every minute. Every second. It's as if her whole life revolves around doing it. And she does a remarkable job of it too, much to her satisfaction.

I'm Maryam, and I'm short-tempered generally, but with my sister Faria, it's 'especially'. She's sixteen, and we have two brothers, Umar and Abdur-Rahman. Umar is nine, and Abdur-Rahman is five. I love both of them 'normally', but if you have brothers you know how annoying they can be sometimes... nonetheless I would do absolutely anything for them, and I know they love me too.

Faria is a bit of a distant one, she never really sits with us, or plays with the 'boys' as my mum calls them. I call her the 'Black Sheep' of the family.

In my mums words, me and Faria are the 'girls', and Umar and Abdur-Rahman are the 'boys' (obviously mum...).

So, my ultra-boring life revolves around playing with the 'boys', and avenging Faria.

My mum's a housewife and my dad's a manager at a local store. My mum accepted Islam when she was nineteen, and my dad's an African-Muslim who came to the UK when he was a child, and so their life began and they had us, four mixed-race children. Faria with her green eyes, me with my black, Umar with his dirty blonde hair, and Abdur-Rahman with his curls. Weird huh?

"Maryam, have you done your homework yet?" Mum popped her head round my door.

"Yes mother, I have completed my utterly interesting task of writing about the life of Victorian England. May I now eat?"

My mum had this... 'rule.' She wouldn't let us eat unless we had done our homework. I guess it worked, and we always managed to get our work done on time. But hey-ho it was stomach time.

She smiled broadly and opened my door wide, "Of course you can."

I happily put my comprehension book and writing pad into my school-bag and headed out. As I was going down the stairs, Faria suddenly came out of nowhere, pushed past me and almost tripped me up. She had already spoiled my mood in the morning by burning my breakfast, and I could feel my temper rising. I went into the kitchen to find my mum.

"Mum, she just tried to trip me up. Tell the weasel to stay away from me!"

"I so didn't mum, she's dreaming again. Aren't you Maryam?" Faria sneered. "Look at the way she said it mum, it's what she was revising upstairs in her room, 'Mum, she just tried to trip me up. Tell the weasel to stay away from me.'"

Faria mimicked me word to word. I had to admit, she sounded just like me when she mimicked me. My mum smiled, probably wanting to laugh at the 'joke'.

"Faria, don't try to trip your sister up please." My mum's voice was too 'normal', it didn't sound like she was telling her off. This wasn't fair!

"Mum! You never believe me! You always think I'm making things up!" I shouted loudly. I was so fed up of all this.

"Maryam, I wasn't there so I can't say she did or she didn't. You say she does something, and then she says she doesn't. What am I supposed to believe huh?"

"You're supposed to believe the one that tells the truth!"

I stormed out of the kitchen. I wasn't hungry anymore. My phone vibrated, it was a message from Hannah,

"Want 2 go 2 the park? I need a break."

I replied back instantly,

"Yes pls, c u thr in 10 mins."

Perfect. I needed a break too. I was the 'joke' in my house. And it hurt me real bad. I texted the third musketeer, Saara,

"Park in 10 mins? I NEED TO ESCAPE FROM HERE."

I didn't wait for her reply and went upstairs to get my abaaya on. I walked as fast I could to the park nearby. We always hung out there, it felt good. Just me, Saara and Hannah. We were worlds apart in appearance. A mix of Asian, White and Black with genes from around the world, but inside, we were like soul-sisters.

The three of us could talk about anything and everything.

Chapter 2

I got back home a little while later because the forces of nature had arrived and wet our hijab covered heads!

Everybody was waiting for me in the dining room, somehow aware that my trip to the park would be short-lived. I noticed my uncle Haamid leaning against the sofa, and I smiled like a Cheshire cat as I quickly went towards him.

"Maryam! Ya Salaam! You've grown so much in the last three months!"

I laughed and hugged uncle as he stood up to meet me. Uncle Haamid had moved to Wales because of work over two years ago, but still came to visit us every few months and it was always a pleasure when he came. He didn't have to bring us presents, but his presence in our house for just that short weekend was enough to refresh us all and bring smiles to our faces. There was never a dull moment with uncle.

Faria was in my direct line of view and I saw her mouth to me, "Yeah, grown fat that is!"

I gave her evils and then smiled at uncle as he pulled back. "I didn't even know you were coming! And I notice that you're growing a beard uncle! It really suits you."

He laughed and stroked his overgrown stubble.

"Yeah, a man realises when he has to change his ways Maryam. I should have grown this thing a long time ago like your dad, but I didn't have the sense. It's just a part of the fresh start I'm going to make *insha Allah.*"

He turned to look at my dad, and then sat back down on the floor.

"Years of you giving me advice have finally kicked in. I've started praying regularly at the Masjid too."

My dad smiled a super-wide smile, and I saw a spark in his eyes. "*Maasha Allah* Haamid! I'm happy you're realising how important these things are."

"Yes bro, what can a man do. A man like me, when there's no wife, there's no life!

That's what I thought anyway. But there is a life, beyond everything else. That life we live for nobody but Allah."

My aunty had died over two years ago. Ever since then, my uncle had spiralled downwards. He had loved her a lot. He completely broke down and his life went out of control. He tried all kinds of things to rid himself of his sadness. He was on depression tablets, started smoking, lost his job because he wouldn't go to work, stayed indoors all the time watching films, thinking that it would help him stop thinking about her. He had even tried committing suicide once, by taking an overdose. Allah protected him *alhamdulillah*.

Aunty Haajar was lovely. We always used to laugh at their names and asked them if they had changed their names to match each other's on purpose - Haamid and Haajar. They had been married for about five years, and had no children. She had died in a car crash while she was travelling with a friend - a drunkard had smashed straight into them. My uncle was traumatised, because he and the friend's husband were in the car behind them and saw everything. They were all coming home from a wedding. The fire team had to cut the car to take my aunty and her friend out, but it was too late and she died on the spot. The friend managed to survive *alhamdulillah*. It was such an upsetting period.

My dad tried really hard to get him to realise that he needed to concentrate on the greater meaning of life.

"Your life can't stop by someone leaving you temporarily,
you need to pick yourself up Akhi, you are going to be with her again one day,
you know that, so why cry and get depressed?"

They were my dad's words to him every single day. I used to get confused at first and would wonder how he would be with her again, but then realised my dad was talking about Heaven and how one day, when my uncle dies too, he would be joining her *insha Allah*.

The truth was, he needed a change of scenery, and so my mum arranged for her brother to give him a job in his company in Wales, and uncle had been working there ever since.

He always says to my mum, *"I will forever be indebted to you for getting me back on my feet sis."*

My uncle is one of the sweetest men I have ever known, and I love him to bits.

Noise was in full flow in the dining room as we all began pouring food for ourselves and catching up with uncle. Yahya and Ibrahim were ecstatic to see him and were going to play football in the park with him later.

Just as the roasted chicken and hot fries had been put in my plate, Faria suddenly asked, "Uncle, are you not going to marry again?"

Everyone froze. The room stilled. My mum was putting a dish of vegetables down on the floor, and she stopped mid- way, looking up at Faria.

"Faria!" my dad's voice boomed. He looked at her with an expression of absolute annoyance. Oh boy, he was angry.

"Sorry... was just thinking..." she looked down, embarrassed. And so she should be. I mean what possessed her to say such a stupid thing in the first place? Besides, when has she ever thought about marriage anyway!

Funny thought, Faria getting married. Who would even marry her? Oh boy, she'd have to move away. I secretly smiled to myself. I couldn't wait until that day... ha ha!

CHAPTER 3

The rest of the weekend passed in a blur.

Things were quiet and normal. Hannah came over on Sunday, and we played with Umar's PS3. Exciting times. Saara, the third musketeer couldn't come. She had some family event going on. Saara was fortunate *maasha Allah* - she had a big sister who was so nice to her. I wished some of it rubbed off on to my miserable sister.

On Monday morning, Hannah looked seriously upset. On Friday she had been taken home from school and had to leave early because of an emergency. She hadn't really contacted us properly at all. She had texted us the same message saying, **"Do du'aa for Aaliyah"** and that was it. I texted her back saying, **"Wotsup?"** but didn't receive a reply. Saara texted me to tell me she didn't get one either.

Saara and I looked at each other knowingly as we walked to school quieter than usual. Hannah was generally a happy girl, she had never in her life looked so... *down.* Saara was intelligent *maasha Allah*, much more than me anyway, so she broke the ice.

"Hani... are you okay?" Hannah didn't look up as we crossed Tavern Street on our way to school.

"Yep..."

We didn't ask her anything else, and walked quietly to our lessons, each of us deep in thought.

During our lunch break Hannah told us how her baby sister had been diagnosed with Cystic Fibrosis. I felt so sorry for her. I remember she had been upset when Aaliyah was born because she had been an only child and this was something totally new for her, but she was more upset now that Aaliyah was ill.

I began praying for Aaliyah after every salaah. And yes, I pray my five daily prayers! As angry a bird as I am, my mum and dad have always had us up praying salaah since the ages of nine or ten, and I'm proud to say I haven't missed a single one. Fortunately for me, the 'time of month' hasn't come yet. If and when it does, the days I would have to miss are forgiven anyway right? So for now, I've got a clean record of praying salaah, and it's something I'm very happy and proud of, *alhamdulillah*.

"No matter what you do in the day - never miss your salaah!" dad always tells us.

Witch Faria prays too – the one thing I'm proud of her for. She doesn't wear her hijab though - she's always been a bit of a rebel and argues back to my parents. I wish she would understand the importance of it and start wearing it too. She will one day, *insha Allah*.

At the end of the school day I hugged Hannah and told her to let me know if she needed anything. As I said my goodbyes to Hannah and Saara, I turned into Boyl Street, thinking I'd make a change for no real reason, and take the back-street instead. I skipped along thinking about what mum might have cooked for dinner, when I heard a slight noise and clatter.

I stopped and looked ahead, through the back-street of Hausen Street and looked straight at my sister Faria, angrily pointing at and in hushed whispers talking to... a *guy*.

Who on earth was he??

I slid back out of their view so as not to be busted. I got a good look at him - he looked about her age, a little bit taller than her, with a black hoody and navy jeans on. He had a familiar face, I couldn't quite put my finger on it. He reminded me of someone. I looked at Faria again, she looked really angry and was still shouting at him in the quietest whisper she could. He was shaking his head and arguing back. Was he Faria's... *boyfriend?!*

As the thought crossed my mind, a big "astaghfirullah" jumped with it. That was the only explanation, who else could he be! And what a stupid place to meet! And why were they arguing? I had so many questions for Madame Faria. What did she think she was up to!

I stayed there watching them for the next few minutes, until Faria began stomping off up the street. I quickly snuck out the other end, and paused for a minute. Should I ask her directly right now, should I tell my parents, or should I hold on until the time felt right? I just could not believe Faria would do something she knew we weren't allowed to do!

I began walking, immersed in these thoughts, not even realising that the Mystery Man walked right past me outside my house on Furness Lane.

CHAPTER 4

Faria was quiet all evening, and it was totally weird because she hadn't said a single horrible thing to me. I even made some comments to her on purpose to try and get her to say something, but she didn't respond... *Oh no, was I missing her witchy-ness?!*

I texted Hannah and Saara,

"My dreams have come true, Faria's turned into a mute potato ;)"

I finished my homework, and then thought I'd do Faria's usual job of watering our plants in the garden considering she was sulking in her bedroom!

That's when I saw it on the floor. A neat, tidy, unmarked envelope between the wall and the Azaleas.

I picked it up and opened it carefully. In it was a note, written in scrawny boyish writing,

"4pm tomorrow in Vicky's Café. you better be there... PLS Furry"

Urgh, I scowled, *'Furry'!* Who the heck says things like that nowadays? A slow smile spread across my face. Well well - this must be from our mystery man.

"Maryam what are you doing out there?" I heard my mum call.

I quickly stuffed the letter in my cardigan pocket and grabbed the watering can. "I'm just watering the plants mum, I'll be two minutes!"

I smiled to myself again... this should be fun. What should I do, turn up to Vicky's Café and ask him who on earth he thinks he is, or give the note to Faria who I'm *sure* this is for... *nah to the second one.* But I was feeling a little scared about the first one!

I felt like a detective on a mission... I needed to do something, I knew that much, I just didn't know what. I went into the kitchen and washed my hands.

"Did dad shout at Faria for what she said to uncle?" I asked mum as casually as I could.

"I think he had a few words with her yes... I'm assuming that's why she's so quiet," answered mum, putting the milk in the fridge and reaching for her cup of tea for a sip. She always had three cups of tea a day for some reason, this was her third.

"Hmmm... does Faria talk to you about personal problems and things mum?"

My mum turned to me eyeing me carefully. "Not so often, she's always been a little distant and reserved when she wants to be."

She turned around and carried on putting the shopping in the fridge. "Though if you need to talk to someone Maryam, you can always talk to me you know."

I smiled to myself. My mum must be thinking that I've got some huge secret turmoil going on in my head. Well I do - but just not about me. I dried my hands and hugged my mum from behind.

"Yes mother dear, as always, I appreciate your openness and willingness to be my secret confidante. I shall consider our proposal."

I stuck my hand out at her to shake it, as if we were doing some sort of business deal.

"Cheeky!" My mum laughed at my sarcasm and strangeness. She shook my hand just to keep me happy. Yes, strangeness and sarcasm was a natural part of me. I just couldn't help it.

I skipped up the stairs to Faria's room.

"Knock knock," I said, as I pushed her door open without actually knocking.

"What do you want?" she snapped. She was sitting on the bed in her night pyjamas. She closed her laptop screen as I made myself at home on her bean bag.

"Isn't it a bit early, or should I say *late*, to be wearing your night clothes?"

"None of your business."

"Why are you acting so depressed?"

"None of your business."

"Is it because dad told you off for being rude to uncle?"

"I was *not* being rude."

"I think it was rude.

"I don't care what you think."

"We *all* thought it was rude."

She looked at me with a sudden hurt in her eyes. "Well it wasn't. He needs to move on, everybody needs to move on one day, you can't be the same person all your life."

Interesting... she's getting all deep and meaningful now.

"He doesn't want to move on, he wants to remember his wife and keep them memories. If he doesn't want to marry again, that's his choice. Act your age. You shouldn't have said something as insensitive as that to him, when you know how he's just got over it. He tried to commit suicide in memory of her for Heaven's sake Faria. Grow up and understand the way the world works – it's not all as black and white as you think that 'yes, she's now died, let me go and find another one.' He has feelings. People have feelings."

I threw in the last line to see if she'd have a melt down and tell me about her feelings for the mystery man. Instead she looked at the window.

I asked, "Where do you want to move on to?"

She looked back at me squinting. "You what?"

"I'm just asking, you said everybody needs to move on, so where are you moving on from, and to?"

Faria stopped whatever it was that she was going to say. She looked at me with her mouth somewhat open, and then closed it again. Her face had almost dropped in a pained, hurt, sort of way. Then it changed back to her usual moody one.

"Don't you have anything better to do?"

I smiled. "Yes, indeed I do dear sister, indeed I do."

I stood up and walked out checking my phone and chuckling at Saara and Hannah's replies at my earlier text message.

CHAPTER 5

I was excited today.

"So guys, see you at 4.15 p.m. at Vicky's?" I asked cheerfully.

"Yes *insha Allah*," said Saara in her simple, no-nonsense way.

"I won't be able to stay for long, when dad comes from work we're going to the hospital, but yeah I'll see you there and ask dad to pick me up from there *insha Allah*," Hannah answered tiredly.

She looked really worn out. I felt guilty for being so cheerful when she was so upset. Yet I couldn't help it, I was on a Sherlock mission about to uncover some sort of hidden treasure.

I hadn't told Saara or Hannah about my plans, or what had happened with Faria, the mystery man, and the note, because I didn't want to talk about my sister in a negative way. I didn't even know if this guy was her boyfriend, and I didn't want to spread lies about her if it wasn't true. Spreading rumours is completely haram, a lesson Saara always reminded us about when we got over excited about hearing some gossip.

Over-night, I had made plans on what I would do. I decided that I would turn up to Vicky's Café at 4.15 p.m. with Saara and Hannah of course, not that they would know what I'm really there for. I would sit and wait to see who turned up to meet him - Faria's phone was in repair, so he might have emailed her or something if he had her email address. If she turned up, I would confront her there and then about who he was, and involve my parents if my suspicions were true. If she didn't turn up, obviously because I hadn't given her the old-fashioned 'letter', I would still go up to him and ask him who he was. *It was all quite simple really.*

I got home from school, showered, changed, prayed my dhuhr salaah, and loitered around the house for a few minutes before getting out. Vicky's Café was a little out of my way – it was in Dumries, an area near us, and was about a half-hour walk from my house,

44

though it was closer to Saara's and Maryam's by about five minutes or so. I began the walk, making silent prayers that everything would go as planned today, the way I had been planning it in my head all night.

Hannah was already waiting outside the red shacked café, probably because she felt little need to wait inside her empty home. There wasn't anyone in it since her mum and Aaliyah were in hospital, and her dad was at work.

"Hey Hani!" I waved at her as I walked towards her.

She smiled back. Just then Saara joined us.

"Hey you look beautiful *maasha Allah* in that red colour," I said. Saara shyly smiled back.

"And you match Vicky's café as well!" I winked at her and pointed to the red sign. We all laughed and went inside. I needed a spot where I could see everybody and everything in the café. It wasn't hard to find since it was so quiet with only a few customers. We sat at the round centre table. This was a nice place. Really funky and retro.

"How's Aaliyah?" I asked Hannah, whilst analysing how clean the table was. *Spotless.*

"Not good," Hannah looked down at her hands. "Every time I go there are doctors and nurses milling around her. It's when I see mum or dad crying that I feel the worst."

"Hey, you shouldn't feel bad," said Saara. "It's meant to be - her illness is meant to be. It's from Allah, whether it's good or bad. You've just got to pray your hardest, and be at your best. You'll see, things will all work out – they always do."

She touched Hannah's hand affectionately. I loved Saara's wisdom.

"And Hani," I chipped in, "you should make the most of this time to prove to your parents how much you love them. You're all they have right now to cheer them up."

Hannah smiled. "You're right. I need to sort myself out. I always let myself get upset when really, it's my parents who need the support. It doesn't help them if I mope around all day."

"You don't realise how strong your parents are, and how much pain they go through, until something like this happens," said Saara. "You know, sometimes I look at my mum and dad, and just can't believe how they're always in the same good mood, even though I know there are a hundred and one problems in the background. But they do that for us, because they don't want us to be affected by it."

"So true..." I mumbled, thinking of all the fights and arguments my parents have to put up with in our house.

"And on top of all that," continued Saara, "you'll realise how much of a better person and how much stronger you yourself will become, because of all these difficulties and problems. If you patiently come out of this problem, the next one will be even easier. It doesn't help anyone if we cry all day or get depressed. It does help however, if we turn to Allah and ask Him for help. It's not like anyone else can help is it?"

Hannah smiled. "You're right. And you know what, I think we are really blessed *alhamdulillah*, because Aaliyah is slowly recovering - even though it doesn't seem like it for someone else. I've noticed the very slight changes and improvements in her. And it's such a good hospital honestly, the nurses and doctors are amazing. There's one Muslim male nurse there who my dad has become really friendly with, and he's always going above and beyond duty to make sure my mum and Aaliyah are comfortable during the day and at night. It makes you feel so happy when you see such sincere and genuine people trying to help you, even though they don't know you."

"May Allah reward him again and again," said Saara smiling.

I looked at both of them and smiled as well. It was so nice to see Hannah's mood being lifted like this.

I ordered us all fish and chips and we ate quietly. All three of us had fallen into our own deep thoughts; Saara, probably about her parents, though I didn't know what problems they even had because they always were as she said – so happy and normal! Hannah was in deep thought presumably about Aaliyah and her parents, and my thoughts automatically fell to my parents and how they had looked out for all of us all our lives, despite all the fighting and squabbling me and Faria did.

Faria. The name suddenly reminded me of my reason for sitting here, and just as I whizzed my head to the right to face Vicky's red door, he walked in.

There he was, all nerves and guilt. My eyes were glued on him as he quickly scanned the café for a sign of my sister. He sat on a table for two people to our left. Brilliant, he was in my line of vision. Maryam had her back to him, and he was on Saara's right but she hadn't noticed him either.

The day he left the letter I wondered why he didn't just text her - then I remembered that Faria's phone was in repair. So really, there'd be little chance he'd be able to tell her to turn up except through the letter or email, because Faria had Tuesday's off college as well.

My big plan was bound to succeed. I sat and waited, and waited. Saara and Hannah kept talking, and we had even finished our food, but my mind was elsewhere. Hannah got up to leave, it was 5 p.m. *Already?*

"See you tomorrow morning *insha Allah*." She stood to get her bag, "Keep doing du'aa for Aaliyah please."

We gave our goodbyes, hugged her, and she left.

I turned to look at my other best friend in front of me.

"Saara..." I said conspiratorially, "Do you know who that guy is?" I pointed to my left.

Saara hadn't even noticed he was there. She turned once to look, turned back to me, and then quickly turned to him a second time. Blood drained from her face. She froze, as if in shock, watching Mystery Man on his phone tapping his feet impatiently. Almost twenty minutes had passed since he arrived and obviously, Faria hadn't.

"Saara...?" I looked at her, and then back at him - busy on his phone.

Saara quickly put her right hand on the side of her head trying to block her face from him seeing her.

Why?!

"Don't let him see me. Tell me if he comes near us."

"Saara! Who is he, what's going on?" I whispered as quietly as I could.

Great, I thought Saara would be asking *me* the questions, but instead it was me asking her!

"Long story - can we get out?"

Ok this hadn't quite gone to plan.

"Saara just tell me!" I whispered as quietly but as loudly as I could to emphasise that I needed to know.

"Not here, I can't. Finish your food, c'mon."

Just as I tried walloping the last few chips in my mouth, Mystery Man's phone rang.

"She's not here. I knew it! Get the car ready, I'm taking her with me today. I've had enough of this. I'll pick it up at 6."

What was all that about? Was he taking my sister somewhere? Was he kidnapping her? Where were they going to go? Oh my word – *kidnapping!*

My eyes widened to an extent I thought was impossible.

"Hurry *up*," said Saara with urgency.

Just as I was eating the last chip Mystery Man got up.

"He's getting up," I said to her. "Stay where you are, let him leave, we don't have to."

He walked right past our table and out the door, slamming it shut behind him. He hadn't even noticed us or looked in our direction. *Phew.*

Saara's eyes followed him through the window as he crossed the street and disappeared.

"Well," I said huffing, "*that* was interesting. Now what was all *that* about?"

Saara fidgeted with her fingers nervously in front of her. This was the first time I had seen her so... unprepared and... *frightened?* Who on earth *was* this person?

"He's my brother."

CHAPTER 6

Holy moly.

I looked at her horrified. "Your *brother*?"

She nodded.

"I don't understand, how is he your..."

"Before my mum and dad got married, my dad had already been married to somebody else. They had a son together – Idrees. Idrees was a few years old when his mum walked out on them, most likely unknowingly, because she was ill. She sort of ran away. I think some time later she was found and hospitalised. I've never got to the bottom of it because dad doesn't like talking about it. She was depressed, she was a danger to him and to my dad, and so I suppose it helped them when she went as well. Some of her tendencies seemed to rub off on to Idrees because he was a little aggressive and, well... violent too."

"So he's your half brother?" I asked quizzically.

She nodded and rubbed her hands together as if they were cold, then sighed.

"My mum and dad got married, and then a year later they had big sis, Saalihah. Idrees was obviously still living with my dad, and my mum accepted him as her own child. Then Umar was born, and me, and then Abdur-Rahman. When Idrees was in high school, he would be in trouble all the time. I don't remember this of course but Saalihah and Umar remember some bits, and my parents told me other bits. He would fight all the time and was very ill mannered and aggressive. My dad even took him to counselling sessions but he would purposely not be at home when it was time to go, and things like that. Eventually, him and dad started fighting. *A lot*. Once he even hit my dad, and a few times swore at and nearly hit my mum. It got too much for my parents and their patience was wearing thin. He would abuse us a lot as well, shout, swear, be mean to us. Kind of like what you're always saying Faria does, but much, much worse."

"What was the worst thing he ever did to you?" I asked horrified.

She looked at me, nervousness of whether she should say or not clearly on her face.

"He kicked me down the stairs once."

"Oh... no way!" I shouted out really loudly.

Saara looked around slightly embarrassed. "Yeah... he would lock us up in rooms, naughty, silly stuff like that. When he pushed me down the stairs though, that was the last straw. My dad told him he was going to report him to the police and he couldn't handle him ruining everybody's lives. There was just no controlling him. We knew he had ADHD but this was really extreme. Anyway, when he was sixteen he walked out of our house himself. He told my dad he was going, and never coming back. And he really never did come back."

"And you've never seen him again?"

"No... Well, not until today." Saara looked down.

I could tell she was in some sort of shock. As was I. So much information to take in!

"Wow, this is... *insane*. How hard must it have been on your dad to have to deal with a kid who openly beats up his other kids!"

"Yeah," Saara mumbled. "It was like being stuck between a rock and a hard place... Should he keep us safe, and report him, when we're all his children, or should he let him stay in the house and harm everyone else? It was tough."

She looked at me with sadness in her dark brown eyes. "Do you get it, he wasn't just a nasty big brother, he was evil, insane, mad! This is why I say to you Maryam, always, always, be grateful to Allah for what you have, because somebody else out there, has it much harder, and much less, and much worse. We got away from him - or well, he chose to leave us. But how many people out there can't escape from an abusive mum, dad, brother or sister. All sorts goes on out there in the world."

"I also now understand why you and your family are so close.. because you've been through so much."

I reached out across the table and squeezed her hand. She closed her eyes and put her head down, as if she was about to cry. My heart was about to break seeing her like this. I squeezed her hand tighter, not letting go.

50

"Are you going to tell your mum and dad that you've seen him?"

"I don't know. I really don't. They'll be happy to know he's okay, alive and well, because they've not heard from him since he left - but it's going to break their hearts to think he's nearby but hasn't contacted them, or that he might be around to harm us again. I mean, no one even knows where he's been all these years. This all happened ten years or so ago."

"So that means he's... twenty six years old?" I asked, surprised for some reason.

"Yeah." Saara looked up at me, "I wonder where he's living, or what he's doing with his life right now. In ten years a lot can happen. I wonder if he's changed."

I frowned. "Saara... Remember I asked you who he was?"

She looked up at me remembering how this whole saga started.

I carried on, "I've seen Idrees with Faria."

Saara gasped. "How? What do you mean, where have you seen them?"

I quickly recapped the entire story of the back street, the letter, and then remembered it was in my pocket so took it out and showed her. I then told her what my reason was for coming here, and filled her in on what I had heard him saying on the phone, which she didn't catch.

Saara slumped back in her chair. "Oh my days Maryam."

"Oh our days Saara. What are we going to do? Look this hasn't quite gone to... *plan*," I said rubbing my hand over my forehead. "I was going to confront him here, now, while he was sitting here. Now you've said who he is, I don't even *want* to confront him that's for starters, but secondly, it's too close to home. I'm surprised he doesn't recognise me, or you, or even has the guts to be back in town."

Saara's mind had switched to plan mode – I could see it on her face instantly. I knew she'd have a solution, she always worked her way out of mess.

"Is Faria at home?"

I nodded, "She should be yeah."

Saara got up, grabbing her jacket from the back of the chair. "Come on, let's go."

Chapter 7

My heart was pounding.

I ran upstairs to Faria's room with Saara. She wasn't there.

"Mum, where's Faria?" I shouted from the top of the stairs down to my mum who was reading a book in the sitting room.

"She went out about an hour ago. Why, what's wrong?" she shouted back up.

"Oh... nothing really, just wanted to ask her something."

I turned to look at Saara. "Now what?"

"I've got a little while, let's wait and see if she comes back in time."

We waited for about two hours, until 7 p.m.

I lay on my bed staring at the ceiling. "Where *is* she?"

Saara was sitting on my inflatable sofa. She struggled her way out of the inflatable mess and straightened her abaaya.

"I've got to go Maryam, I have to pick the kiddos up from Madrassah. Text me when she gets back, we'll have to talk to her tomorrow."

"What are you going to do about your parents?" I asked.

"I'm going to keep it a secret until we talk to Faria *insha Allah*. I can't rush this with them. I need to know why he's here, and what he's doing with your sister. He might mean no harm, but... I don't know." She sighed. "I'll be off, take care sis. Text me as soon as she's home yeah. I can't help but be a little worried." She frowned.

I walked Saara to the door. I realised that I too was a little worried about where Faria was. It was unlike her to be out for so long. As we went downstairs I saw my mum sitting on the sofa staring at the time frowning, and my dad pacing up and down, still in his work clothes.

"Maryam, Saara, any idea where Faria is? The girl is in *big* trouble when she gets back.

I can't believe she's not told us where she was going!" My dad sat down on the other sofa exasperated.

"No idea dad, sorry... we wanted to ask her something as well and been waiting for her," I answered apologetically. I didn't like seeing my parents this... *concerned*.

"Take care uncle and aunty, I'll ask Saalihah if she's seen at her at college or knows anything, I'll call Maryam and let her know straight away if that's the case."

Saara smiled at my parents, and they smiled back. My mum got up to hug her goodbye and told her to give salaam to her parents.

As Saara closed the front door, my dad stood up to leave and pick the boys up from Madrassah. I sat down next to my mum.

"Mum... Don't you think Faria's been acting really... *off* lately? Do you think she's angry at something, or upset?"

"I don't know what goes on in your teenager brains," said my mum rubbing her cheeks. "I wish I knew."

Guilt was splashed all over my face as I realised I hadn't told my parents what I knew about the Mystery Man. I suddenly felt that right now, the time was right for me to tell her. I wouldn't tell my mum about the connection with Saara, because that was up to Saara to declare to her family first, but I had to tell her about the fact that I had seen Faria with someone and... *oh my word*... the words I had heard him say over the phone sprung to my mind:

> *"She's not here. I knew it! Get the car ready, I'm taking her with me today.*
> *I've had enough of this. I'll pick it up at 6."*

"Mum..." I turned to look at her as my jaw dropped open.

"Assalaaaaaaaaaammmu alayyykum!" Abdur-Rahman's voice burst through the door.

"Wa'alaykumussalaam my little baby, how was Madrassah today?"

My mum stood up, picked him up in a hug and took his bag off him.

My dad followed with Umar. I needed to tell my mum and dad - I felt it with such urgency. I couldn't let this moment pass.

"Mum, dad, I need to tell you something that may be really important for you to know... I think these two should go somewhere else..." I whispered the last part, indicating toward the boys.

My mum and dad both turned to look at me with a knowing look, knowing that I was going to mention something about Faria.

"Umar, Abdur-Rahman, why don't you go to the front room and play the PS3 or something for a bit before it's time for bed?"

They cheered happily as dad opened the door for them without looking at them, his eyes still fixed on me as I stuck my hands in my pocket, nervous. I couldn't figure out what he was thinking - it was making me nervous. I deserved to be nervous though, I was hiding something really important from them. It could have made all the difference a few hours ago, if they had kept Faria at home and not let her go out - to wherever she was right now.

Oh no... What if Faria was hurt, kidnapped, taken to some far away land! What if I never saw her again! My heart felt as if it would fall to the ground, and I swallowed trying to get some air into my lungs, realising that I hadn't breathed since my dad sent the boys to the front room.

"Sit down Faria," mum ordered as both of them came and sat in front of me.

"What is it baby girl?" dad asked, "If it's something about Faria, you know we need to know."

I loosened my hijab nervously. It was suddenly so hot in the room.

"I...err..."

I told them the full story. How I had seen them in the back street, how Faria had been almost shouting at him, how he had left the letter, how I had turned up to the café, and how I had heard him saying those horrifying words.

My mum was frozen with shock. My dad was glaring at me.

"Why did you not tell us before Maryam? Do you know what could happen right now!"

He stood up, angry, rubbing his hands over his recent bald.

"What does this guy look like? I'm going to call the police Maryam, and you need to tell them *everything* you've just told us, do you understand? Do *not* miss out a single detail!" He grabbed the cordless home phone.

"Oh Maryam..." my mum was shaking. "Faria's been kidnapped... Faria... my baby girl's been kidnapped!" My mum had tears streaming down her face.

"What? Mum no! She might not be... look... there's something else..." I knew I had to tell them about him being Saara's half brother.

Just then, there was a sharp rap on the door. My parents looked at each other and then my dad shot to the door to open it, dropping the cordless back in its' place.

"Assalamu 'alaykum akhi, ukhti, how are you!" Saara's mum rushed in, followed by Saara's dad, Saara, and then her elder sister Saalihah.

Saara's dad put his hand on my dad's shoulder. "Akhi Sulaiman, we know everything about Faria... we need to tell you something. Sit down, please."

My dad seemed to shake, as if he was expecting the worst news possible. He was good friends with Saara's dad, my mum was good friend's with her mum, as I was with Saara. Saalihah also went to college with Faria so they knew of each other. I think it was comfort for my parents that their friends had come over, as it was for me when I saw Saara. I ran up to her and held on to her arm, squeezing it in affection. She turned around and to my surprise, hugged me.

"Don't worry," she said, "I told them about Idrees. Have you told yours?" she whispered to me.

"Yeah, I haven't told them about who Idrees is though," I whispered back.

She nodded, grateful that I had stuck to my promise.

"Aunty, uncle, the guy me and Maryam saw in the café... the one who she saw with Faria the day before... he's..." she looked to her parents for encouragement. I saw her father nod at her gently, and she carried on. "It's Idrees."

"*What?*" my dad cried out incredulously.

"Idrees, your son?" my mum asked Saara's dad, with the same aghast look on her face.

"Yes, it's him," Saara's dad, uncle Hamza, answered quietly. "But don't worry, it has worked out to our advantage that we know who he is. Now it's just a matter of finding out where they are. We know they're somewhere together, we just need to know with who, and where, and then we can determine why..." he looked down as if in embarrassment.

I could only imagine how difficult it must have been for him to accept the fact that his violent, run-away son had possibly *kidnapped* his friend's daughter. My parents knew everything about Idrees' past.

He continued, "Saalihah said she knows for definite that her friend Hafsah's elder brother lent his car to someone they call 'Iddy' earlier on today... we can assume we know who 'Iddy' is. I've spoken to Hafsah's uncle, I know him well. He's asking details from the boy as we speak, and said he'll call me as soon as he's finished speaking to him."

"Did you know that Idrees was back in town?" my dad asked uncle Hamza, whilst pointing to the sofa, indicating for him to sit down.

Saara's mum, aunty Zahra, was sitting next to my mum on the other sofa, and at that point I realised me, Saara and Saalihah were all still standing as well, so I pulled the floor cushions out for us all to sit down. I had forgotten my manners in all the rush.

"No," uncle Hamza said. He cleared his throat. "I had no idea."

"Don't worry uncle," Saalihah chirped in looking at my dad, "It won't be hard to find out where they are. Hafsah told me that apparently this 'Iddy' is an 'old friend' of her brother's. That's why her brother is so excited at him coming back suddenly and so he's doing him favours to keep him here... He might not know where they've gone, but we'll have the registration plate. She also told me that she's pretty sure he works in the hospital, as a nurse."

"Jaabir is on duty tonight, I've sent him a message to find Idrees' name, where he works, what days, and what exactly he's doing here." Jaabir was a family friend of both mine and Saara's families, and a doctor at the hospital.

"Wow, Idrees a nurse?" my mum asked, shocked.

"Yeah, who would have thought..." aunty Zahra said. "It makes me think that he may have changed after all, *insha Allah*."

"I pray to God that he has..." scowled uncle Hamza.

CHAPTER 8

The evening passed quickly.

Saalihah and me made tea for everyone, while mum put the boys to bed. My dad kept worrying about it being a school night but me and Saara made it clear we weren't going to be able to sleep until this problem was dealt with.

Hafsah's uncle rang to tell us that his nephew definitely *had* lent the car to Idrees, and that he was only going to borrow it for a few hours. They also definitely *didn't* intend to run away as Idrees had work the next day, and was expecting him to return it later on in the night. He also said that Faria knew she was going to go with him to visit someone, and he hadn't kidnapped her or done anything crazy like that! I thought that was a little odd, how did he get in touch with Faria when she had no phone etc? And who did they go to visit?

After all this new information however, I was relieved. Before this, I had been having visions in my head of him putting a sack over her head and bundling her into the back of a car. *Dramatic.* Idrees wasn't answering his phone though, so Hafsah's brother had no idea what was going on and what time they would be back.

It was 10 p.m.

Dr Jaabir rang uncle Hamza and told him that there was indeed a nurse by the name of Idrees Ali who had recently began work at the hospital, and was usually working in the children's ICU. He had, of course, had all background checks done on him before he got the job, and said everything was clear. There were no criminal records, and he was actually qualified! He had been working in a Manchester hospital before here, and was reliable, trustworthy, punctual - everything was violent-free and... *normal.*

Saara's parents looked confused as they struggled to digest the information. It was as though Idrees was a completely different person.

"Then again it has been over ten years dad... he might now be the son you always wanted him to be," Saara said thoughtfully.

That made me smile. Saara still thought the best of Idrees, even though he had physically abused her so many times as a child. I would have been scarred forever if I was in her place.

"We still don't know where they are, and why she's not coming *home*," my mum said quietly, sighing.

She was emotionally drained from crying all evening. I was struggling to hold back my tears as well, but I managed to. I can't cry in front of other people. *Just one of them things.*

The adults had unanimously decided not to involve the police yet - according to my dad they would be little use considering both Faria and Idrees are considered adults, and we were expecting them back home at some point. My dad said we should wait until midnight at the latest, and if they weren't back by then, it wouldn't be difficult for the police to track the car anyway. Plus, we were holding on to the idea that Idrees had work in the morning, so we could always go and grab him at the hospital in the morning. Apparently he was working a double shift tomorrow.

Saara and I got a text from Hannah just then, both our phones pinged and dinged at the same time. My face lit up thinking about Hannah. I wished she was here too.

"They're going to let Aaliyah come home 2morrow :)"

"Hey everyone, Hannah said they're letting Aaliyah come home tomorrow!" I beamed.

I was so, so happy for her. There was a murmur of *alhamdulillah's* and *maasha Allah's* from everyone, and for a few minutes everyone else's faces lit up as well.

I quickly texted her back with congratulations. I didn't mention what was going on though, I wasn't going to burden her with our problems - she had just come out of hers, *alhamdulillah.*

Just then, we heard a creak, as the front door knob began to turn...

CHAPTER 9

Faria froze and looked around the room, as she opened the living room door.

"Faria!" my mum yelled, rising from her chair abruptly.

"Where on *earth* have you been young lady?" dad bellowed from the windowsill. "Do you know how worried we've been? Do you even know what *time* it is!" He was super angry...

Faria said nothing. Her face was bright red and she just stared at the carpet, frozen with one hand on the door handle, and the other holding her satchel. She looked like she had been crying. *I actually felt really sorry for her.*

I quickly got up, rushed toward her, and hugged her. Spur of the moment action - I really don't know what possessed me. I hadn't ever hugged her before. Yuck. Faria looked horrified, as if I had committed a sin. But she didn't push me off, she actually dropped her satchel on the ground and wrapped one arm around my back.

"Sit down big sis," I whispered to her, almost about to burst out crying myself. My heart went out to her. She reluctantly let go of the door handle and sat in my place on the floor, on the cushion next to Saara.

I closed the door and quietly went and sat down on the other side of her. My parents still hadn't approached her − I knew they were deciding in their minds as to what they should do - show her affection, or show her exactly how knee deep in trouble she was? They were both staring at her with unreadable faces, waiting for her to say something.

We all were.

"Are you okay Faria?" Saalihah asked smiling softly.

Faria nodded, and wiped a slow moving tear from her face. "I'm sorry dad... mum... everyone," she sniffled quietly. "I... I should have got back ages ago. I just..." she mumbled quietly, and then fell silent.

"Where's Idrees?" asked uncle Hamza.

Faria looked up surprised, but didn't ask how he knew about him. I suppose she didn't dare ask, considering she was the one who needed to answer questions right now.

"He's gone - back to his flat."

"Where's his flat?"

She looked up and knew from the look on uncle Hamza's face that she had to tell him whether she'd like it or not.

"23a Park Street, just off Shetland Drive."

"Huh, Abdullah's house?" My dad looked at Saara's dad, and they both frowned.

Abdullah was Hani's dad. He was a property developer, and had a number of properties that he had bought himself and would rent out.

"Abdullah, as in Hannah's dad?" I asked to make sure.

My dad nodded. "He owns 23 Park Street, flat a and b. How could Idrees have got in and afforded that one, it's expensive!" He rubbed his bald head again, exasperated.

Uncle Hamza still had a frown on his face. He took his phone out of his jacket pocket and began calling someone - I assumed it was Hannah's dad. We all heard the ringing tone, and I realised everyone in the room was leaning in, trying to listen to what was being said next.

"Assalaamu alayk, Abdullah! Alhamdulillah. How is Aaliyah? We've heard the good news, I'm really happy she's coming home tomorrow."

We couldn't make out what Hani's dad was saying but he must have had a smile on his face. He was such a lovely man - one of my favourite uncles.

"Listen, sorry to call you so late bro, I need to ask you something very important... your flat, 23a Park Street? Who's living in it now?"

At that moment, uncle switched it on loudspeaker. I heard the soft voice of uncle Abdullah coming through the phone. He sounded tired.

"It's a lad who's recently moved into the area, Idrees Ali. He's a nurse at the Royal. He's been one of the nurses looking after Aaliyah. I've got chatting to him quite a few times, he was looking for a place and I appreciate everything he's done for our baby. He seems like a good lad, struggling to make his way in life, as we all have done, so I went with my gut feeling and offered it to him at a reduced price. He was having to commute an hour and a half to the hospital every day on bus, and Park Street's round the corner from the hospital so... Why, what's happened? Did you need the flat for something or someone?"

"*Idrees Ali...* I'll fill you in very soon Abdullah, don't worry, I just needed to make sure - it's someone I know. I'll come and see you tomorrow evening *insha Allah.* You get lots of rest bro, you've got a happy day ahead of you tomorrow!" Uncle Hamza smiled and hung up.

I felt so happy inside thinking about how these friends wouldn't burden each other with their problems. Because of Aaliyah being ready to come home, Saara's dad didn't want to put his own child's problems on uncle Abdullah's shoulders. They were so wise *maasha Allah.* It reminded me of me, Saara and Hannah. Maybe that's why we were always so considerate of each other's feelings - because we saw our father's being that way.

"Faria, did he hurt you?" Uncle Hamza turned to face Faria.

"No!" Faria exclaimed, "Idrees isn't like that, he..."

"How did you get to know him?" my dad asked Faria sharply.

Faria went quiet.

"Ok Faria, tell me something, why has he been contacting you? Did you know you were going to meet him, or did he just turn up?" asked uncle.

"I knew we were going to meet... We needed to talk and he wanted me to meet someone, so..." she cleared her throat. "So, we went and..." she looked around nervously.

"We want to get married!" she exclaimed.

CHAPTER 10

I didn't hear a single person in the room breathing.

"Say that again?" said my mum.

Tears started pouring down Faria's face. "We want to get married, I really, really like him Ma, I promise we've not done anything bad, he only wanted to meet me to tell me to talk to you guys!" she carried on babbling. "He's so respectful, so caring, so considerate, he's building a life for himself, I don't want someone who messes about or is immature like the other guys at college, Idrees is perfect for me!"

"Idrees... Idrees is..." Uncle Hamza rubbed his hands through his hair exasperated, "You two want to get *married?*"

"Yes uncle, I was going to talk to mum and dad today. I've told him I didn't think they'd agree because they never mention marriage to me and I'm scared of bringing it up. And then mum keeps talking about uncle Huzaifah's son who lives in London, and I've always thought she's hinting at me to marry him!"

My mum stared at Faria as if she had offended her. "Uncle Huzaifah's son is *twice* your age Faria, why would I ask you to marry him! Have some sense you silly girl!" she shouted.

"Well I didn't know that Ma, what else would I think. You're always bringing him up when I'm sitting there, asking me what I think, and then Idrees - he keeps telling me to at least *try* with you. My phone didn't mess up, it's not in repair, I just stopped using it because I needed time to *think!* From everyone at home, from Idrees, from myself even! But it worked, and I have thought, and I've realised I do really want to do this! I'm not interested in college or anything else, I just want to settle down, and have a family!"

"You *dare* try leaving college young lady!" my mum shouted suddenly.

"Faria, why did you not tell us this before! I hate to admit but Idrees was right, you should have at least *tried!*" My dad stood up and walked to the window again. He always seemed to stand there when he was angry. "You do *not* just go somewhere with a boy, who by the way is *not* your mahram, who it is *haram* for you to be with, and then think that it's perfectly okay and your parents will understand! Tell me, where have me and your Ma gone wrong? What is it that we've not taught you about manners, about respect, about Islam! About the way a Muslim girl should *behave*! Do you even know who Idrees really is? I mean did it never cross your mind that we'd find out one day!"

My dad was shouting at the top of his lungs. No body dared breathe louder than necessary. I had never, *ever*, seen my dad this enraged. Fortunately, Umar and Abdur-Rahman were in bed and our house was pretty well sound proofed. Saara's brothers were at home with their aunty. The kids would have been terrified seeing dad like this. *I* was terrified.

"I didn't think you'd agree... Dad I already *know* he's uncle Hamza's son... I know what he used to do when he was younger, he's told me everything. I knew you'd say no," she whispered, almost heartbroken. "This is what I was scared of..."

"You damn right better have been scared before you tell me you *dared* try meeting boys in secret!" my dad shouted back smacking his hand against the wall.

Everyone in the room was deadly silent, only my dad's loud breathing could be heard. As I said, he was seriously angry, and I understood why. He felt betrayed. He had given us everything we could have ever asked for, but had always told us to safeguard ourselves and be good Muslim girls. He especially told us that girls shouldn't mess about or mix with non-mahrams. The reality stung me of how serious the situation was. I promised myself that I would never, ever, betray my father's trust, and never get involved with a guy before marriage. *Insha Allah.*

"Why did he not tell me he was back?" uncle Hamza asked quietly.

I noticed he had tears in his eyes. *Oh my word.* I wanted to cry as well.

"He was... scared... scared that you'd be scared of him. Scared that aunty would not let him near her again. Scared of what he's done to your kids, and that you might report him," she answered.

"Oh and marrying you is going to solve all the problems?" aunty Zahra added horrified. "Did he not think of what *that* would do! As if you two would be able to marry and we wouldn't know about it!"

Faria looked down, sobbing. "I'm sorry aunty, I didn't think, both of us didn't think... I'm... sorry. Dad... I didn't mean for this to happen..."

"Don't call me *dad*," my dad shouted back, turning his back to her and looking emptily at the window.

I was terrified. Who's side was I supposed to be on? It was as if my sister and dad were in a battlefield. My mum was still silent, thankfully. Faria had messed up big time. I looked at her and she looked so regretful and lonely. Maybe she just needed someone to help her out. I put my arm around her and hugged her tight.

"Whose house did you go to with Idrees? Where did you go?" uncle Hamza asked.

Faria didn't look up at him. She paused for a few second, as if contemplating on an answer. "He took me to see his mum..."

A *massive*, heavy, deadly silence took over the room.

"Are you joking with me? You went to see Husna? Why! How does Idrees even know where she is!" he exclaimed.

"I don't know uncle, honestly! I know he's been looking for her for ages and he just said to me he needs me to meet her, it took ages getting there - I don't even really know where it was!" Faria looked up at him pleading her innocence.

"This is crazy. We need to do something about this. Akhi, we're going home, my brain is in a million places right now. You guys get some rest, it's late, we all have work and school tomorrow, I'll contact you tomorrow and we'll figure something out *insha Allah*."

Saara's dad hugged my dad and their family got up to leave.

It was good timing. We were all really tired.

As soon as they left from the front door, my dad turned to Faria. "I've got serious questions for you tomorrow. I'm so angry right now, that I don't even want to bother talking to you, because I'm afraid I may do or say something I'll regret. You're not leaving this house tomorrow, or ever, until this issue is resolved. And don't get your hopes up Faria, believe me, after what you've just done, it's going to take me a very long time to forgive you." He paused and looked at her sullenly. "My own daughter... how could she..."

As he said this, he shook his head, slammed the living room door shut and went upstairs.

My mum was still where she had been before Saara's family left. She got up, put her hands on Faria's cheeks and kissed her forehead.

"O Faria. Why - *why* would you choose to do things that you know will make our life difficult. Why do you girls make such *unwise* choices?"

She sighed loudly, dropped her hands, and turned to go upstairs. She clearly didn't have any tears left. She was absolutely exhausted.

I sighed to myself quietly and looked at Faria. I wondered what would happen now. Two things I was glad about though were that my sister was safe, and she was home. She stood up and to my surprise, hugged me really tightly.

"Thank you so much Maryam, for being here today," she whispered.

I smiled back and hugged her again.

Maybe she wouldn't be able to marry Idrees, or maybe my parents would never forgive her, but suddenly, I felt this extreme attachment and bond to my sister that I had never felt before.

I truly loved her. Things would be different between us from now on. *I could feel it.*

SAARA

CHAPTER 1

Dear Diary: This is insane. I cannot believe he's back. Idrees. After everything that happened. he decides to return. Dad promised us he wouldn't come back. Mum hugged me and Saalihah the day he locked us in the cellar and we were screaming for help. I remember it so clearly like it was yesterday. Mum cried her eyes out. and told dad to send him away. Dad was torn apart and I know Idrees had heard. because that night he walked out never to come back. And now he's back. Why O Allah?

I closed my diary and slid it under my bed. I lay on my back and sighed loudly. I understood that he was older and probably matured, but I couldn't help feeling a little scared of him even now. I couldn't get the images out of my head, of how he had slapped Saalihah once for not giving him something quick enough, and kicked Ibrahim as a baby. Ibrahim had screamed so hard that I thought he was going to die.

Why would Idrees do things like that? I resigned myself to the fact that I'd probably never know. That's when the thought struck me. Perhaps now, this was the opportunity to find out what used to run through his head.

That's if he came home and talked to us of course. Which was unlikely. From the look on the face of uncle Sulaiman yesterday, there was no chance Faria was ever going to be allowed out the house again, let alone marry Idrees.

"Dad... are you going to go to his flat?" Saalihah had asked while on the way home from Maryam's.

My dad didn't reply. The car sunk into silence again.

I felt so sorry for my dad, my hero, my role model. He was a man of strength, a man of his word. He never said something he didn't mean, and yet he never offended anyone. He went out of his way to help others, and there was nothing he wouldn't do for you if you needed something. He was in a league of his own. And right now he was heart- broken. I couldn't help but feel that we all just needed to give him space, to figure this out for himself. It was after all *his* flesh and blood that was back in town.

Once home, Saalihah and I went straight to our rooms. We were as close as sisters could be - maybe more than other sisters - but it worked for us. She was there for me when I needed her, and I was there for her, even though she was a few years older than me. In all honesty, it was probably because of the incidents with Idrees that we had become so close. We were both scared and fighting against the same evil force when we were younger.

It's funny, because when I saw him in the café with Maryam, I caught a glimpse of him from the side. He just looked like a regular guy who you might see walking around - not somebody who would be so violent and aggressive in his younger days. I didn't look long enough to notice who he was, which I suppose was good, or I would have been out of the café immediately. Maybe he was different after all. People change all the time. Besides, he now had a job as a nurse – that's a caring occupation right... *he must be different.*

I shared these thoughts with Saalihah, but she didn't respond much and just replied with 'hmm' and 'yeah'. She didn't want to talk. I turned the light off and crawled into my bed, exhausted.

School tomorrow. For the first time in a very long time, I really couldn't be bothered to go.

CHAPTER 2

Surprisingly, the next few days passed as normal.

No one mentioned Idrees to my father, though we were all wondering what was going on. Plus, because of the boys being around, we didn't want to say his name. They wouldn't have remembered him much, but then again you never know. Sometimes you have childhood memories that you can't rid yourself of.

School was nothing special, and I couldn't concentrate well because I kept wondering what was going on. Maryam filled me in about how Faria told her parents everything, and how she really, really wanted to marry Idrees. But she didn't dare argue with her parents, and surprisingly stayed quiet as her parents offloaded all their frustration and anger on her for even leaving the house that day and agreeing to see someone who was not a mahram for her, as well as returning so late, worrying everyone at home, putting my family through difficulty, and then to have chosen someone like Idrees to marry, stupidly thinking that nobody would have a problem with it!

I went to Maryam's house a few times but didn't see Faria at all as she was choosing to spend her nights and days locked away in her room. She knew she had done major wrong, so I guess she needed to keep her distance until everyone cooled down. I was really happy though - it seemed that Maryam and Faria had grown closer as sisters. She had opened up with Maryam for the first time, and filled her in on the complications she had experienced with Idrees, as well as the regrets she had.

"I should never have spoken to him. I've finally realised why Islam tells us not to be open and talk to non-mahrams. Shaytaan gets in your head and confuses the life out of you," Maryam had quoted her as saying. Maryam seemed maturer as well, more understanding and more patient. Weeks before this, she would have laughed at Faria and her problems, and even wished for her to get married and get out of her life!

Faria confessed she would end everything with Idrees if her parents, or my parents told her to. I was happy that Faria had become so considerate, and was coming closer to Allah through this. Saalihah went to visit her a few times, and she told me that Faria was spending most of her time praying and reading, and seemed to become more aware and appreciative of Islam and her existence as a Muslim girl.

It can't have been easy to give up someone you really like, for the sake of Allah - but it's worth it. I knew this, and Saalihah was the best to advise Faria right now, because there was someone Saalihah had really liked last year, but she was too decent and didn't approach the guy at all. Later on in the year, he ended up getting involved in drugs and stupid gang-fights. He's now in jail serving a two year sentence. She always tells me, that if Allah doesn't allow something to happen, it's because He's saving you from something, even if you don't know it.

We had filled Hannah in on all the news properly after school on Friday. She had been busy with her sister coming home before that and we didn't want to dampen the mood for her.

"Oh my word you guys, I've seen him *so* many times in hospital, I cant believe that's him! Saara, I'm so sorry for all this, had I known I would have grabbed him and shook him from the collar and told him to do one!" she said exasperated.

"Nah, I'm cool with things. I believe everything happens for a reason, and everything that happens is from Allah, we have to just take a step back and understand the wisdom behind it." I paused for a second. "It's hard to do that sometimes, but it's all a part of the test. Since everything's happened everyone's gone into cave mode and they're sort of praying non-stop, increasing Qur'aan and nafl salaah etc, hoping that Allah has His Mercy on us and makes a way out of this mess. My parents don't know what to do about Idrees, and he's not come to our house yet either. It's affecting their relationship with Maryam's parents too. I can't believe he's being so inconsiderate."

"Same in my house Saara. It's amazing how when something happens, we all turn to Allah immediately. It's good, but interesting because we need to remember Him when we have happy times as well," Maryam added.

"Yeah, I get you both totally. Me and my parents did the same when Aaliyah got ill," said Hannah.

"Make sure you keep up the Fajr salaah, tasbeeh and Qur'aan Hani, don't let it go now just because Aaliyah's back," I advised her.

I knew how easy it was to forget Allah the minute things went back to normal. We always have to have Allah in mind, no matter what the circumstance.

"*Insha Allah,*" Hannah smiled. It felt good to see her so happy again.

"Before all this, dad used to pray salaah at home and sometimes the Mosque, but now he's started going to the Mosque regularly. Mums started praying salaah for a lot longer, and even Faria has started reciting the Qur'aan. I've been trying to look after the boys a bit more than usual, to make it easier on my parents. They just seem to be in their own world," Maryam frowned.

"That is normal though isn't it," said Hannah, "considering they're now worrying about whether to let Faria marry him or not.. I mean, that's the issue now for your family isn't it?"

"Yeah, that's the issue," Maryam said, looking up at me embarrassed.

"Don't feel embarrassed because of me being here Maryam, pretend I've got nothing to do with Idrees. Your family has to consider him just like they would consider anybody else, at the end of the day it's your sister's life on hold, and besides, it's not like he's my real brother or that he went through my dad for the proposal," I reassured her, knowing she was probably a little uneasy talking about Idrees and Faria in front of me, thinking that if they rejected Idrees, they were rejecting us all.

"Yeah... Last night I wanted some milk so I came downstairs around 11 p.m. and saw my parents talking in the living room. I don't know what they were saying but it was obviously about Faria. I just gave my two-pence worth and told them that in my opinion, if Saara's dad agrees, considering Faria's clearly wanting to marry him and no one else, and is so dead and heart broken without him, they should just go for it," said Maryam in a matter-of-fact way. "Besides, I can't imagine anyone else marrying Faria the Witch!"

We all laughed. At least their sister-hate relationship hadn't totally been forgotten!

"I agree," I said. "I'm going to speak to my dad today, see what's happening. He's not visited Idrees yet, I think that's going to be the biggest hurdle for him. Letting him marry Faria, well, I know he'd be overjoyed with that but only if Idrees has changed. Otherwise he wouldn't want her to marry an abusive, horrible person like what Idrees was when he was younger. I guess I think the same - who would marry Idrees!"

Hannah reached over the cream café table to hold my hand, "People change overnight Saara, don't over judge him because of his past. 'Every saint has a past, every sinner has a future', remember?" she smiled.

I smiled back. She was right. I felt a renewed sense of hope and vigour. I wanted this whole saga to be over.

I would talk to Idrees if I had to, find out why he's here, genuinely help him if he wanted change, and tell him to get lost if I had to as well.

CHAPTER 3

"Saara, you're being unrealistic. I *don't* want you to go, I'm being serious," Saalihah was using her pleading voice now.

"Saalihah, I only told you in case I don't get back home before 7 p.m. Just cover my back. If I'm in harm, obviously I won't text you within the hour, so then bring dad and come for me to his flat. Yeah?"

I grabbed my bag and sighed. "Saalihah, he's still our brother. I care for him, whether I want to care or not. I could never hate him. And you and I both can't stand to see dad as upset and worn out as he is right now. He doesn't have the courage to have a stand-off with Idrees, because as much as we don't want to admit it, dad *is* scared of him. You know what he used to do before, and now he's much bigger, much stronger, God knows what he's capable of." I gave her a quick hug.

"Text me as soon as you can, and I swear you better *not* forget to text me within the next hour," she said in her big sister voice.

"Yes I promise madame, I'll see you soon *insha Allah*," I left before she could change her mind.

I told my parents I was meeting a friend and zoomed out, much to my guilt, before they asked any more questions. I couldn't tell them where I was going because I knew they'd stop me. However, I knew I had to do this. He was my half-brother, I had to take this simple step to stop everything that was going on, and make it make sense.

I walked to the bus stop quickly and saw Hannah was already waiting for me. I had asked her to come along. She was a safer option than Maryam because of the Faria situation, and she knew the in's and out's of the area because her dad had a number of properties there as well. We caught the A63 bus and Hannah told me it would take less than fifteen minutes. Hannah knew his working pattern by now and I prayed he would be at home as we expected him to be, and hadn't changed his shifts.

"Do you know what you're going to say to him?" Hannah asked quietly.

"Yes," I breathed out nervously.

We got off the bus.

My heart was racing as we turned into Neville Lane. Park Street was around the corner.

"I'm going to be right outside okay? There's a little bench on the front side, I'll be sitting there, but the flat windows have blinds on them which are usually open in the day time, so if anything happens and if he's about to hit you, you come straight to the front window. I'll be able to see you directly, and the police will be on their way before he can even do anything." She hugged me with concern.

I noticed the bench she was talking about, and I looked up at the flat in front me. A light was on inside. She was right - the blinds were open. I breathed out quietly and went to the front door, suddenly feeling a rush of panic and fear inside me.

You have to do this Saara, you have to do this, I reminded myself.

I paused a second before I rang the doorbell for Flat A. I did it quickly so that I couldn't change my mind. I was seriously panicking now.

What was I even supposed to say to him? I couldn't even remember anything!

A few seconds passed and nothing happened. I lifted my hand to ring the doorbell again but stopped as I heard the lock turning and the door handle slowly opening.

My heart stopped beating.

The door swung open and in front of me stood the boy who had abused, beaten, and sworn at me when I was a kid.

I stopped breathing as I looked up at him.

The first thing I noticed was that he appeared well dressed... 'smartly' dressed even.

Nothing like the angry kid he once was who I imagined would wear torn jeans, a backwards cap, be unclean and not look after himself (*not that there's anything wrong with torn jeans or a backwards cap – of course*).

"Can I help you?" he asked with a frown.

Cor blimey. He didn't recognise me.

I looked up at him and tightened my grip around my bag.

"Idrees?" I asked.

He paused. "Yes?"

"Why are you back in town?"

He paused again, scrutinising me, clearly trying to figure out who I was.

"S... Saara?" Now it was his turn to look almost frightened.

Funny, I wasn't the one who used to beat me up.

I nodded. "I thought... I thought you weren't ever planning on coming back," I managed to say.

He finally let go of the door handle I noticed he was still holding, and rubbed his palm on the back of his neck.

"I, err... I didn't think I was either," he looked at me carefully. He moved away from the doorway and gestured inside, "Do you think we should have any conversation we're going to have *inside* instead of outside?"

I surveyed his face carefully, checking for any signs of anger or violence. I saw nothing but confusion and nervousness.

I wrung my hands together. "Erm, okay, I don't have long," I quickly added.

CHAPTER 4

The first thing I noticed was the smell of food having just been eaten, or cooked. It actually smelt good.

Idrees the cook, *what a funny thought.* I smiled to myself, and quickly dropped my smile as he came into the living room.

"Do you want to err... sit down, somewhere?"

He looked around and quickly grabbed some papers and folders from the sofa, and dumped them on the floor. As I sat down he reached out and grabbed a bean bag from a corner, and sat on the opposite side of the room.

"Okay... this is awkward. How did you know I was here?" he asked.

"Well it's hardly going to stay a secret is it, considering you're prancing around with Faria," I bit back.

He looked at the laptop that was on the table in front of him, embarrassed. I wasn't going to let him have the privilege of knowing how we know things. *He* was the one who needed to answer the questions.

"Did you come back in town for Faria?" I made a guess that they had known each other way before he came back into town.

He paused. "Not entirely, I came back for work, but she was part of the reason."

There was an awkward silence and then he said, "I can't believe you've grown so much Saara."

"Well that's what people do isn't it Idrees, they grow up. Have you grown up?"

His face flushed into a deep red, and he stuttered, "I... I have, yeah... I'm really sorry Saara, for everything I did when we were kids. I honestly can't believe I was that person. I don't know what was wrong with me. I really am sorry."

I felt happy at his apology, at least he cared to apologise. I added a tick in the *'Idrees has changed'* column in my head.

"Why have you not come home to see dad?" I asked.

"How can I see a man who hates the sight of my face?" he scowled.

"If he hates the sight of you, it's because of what *you* did, not because of anything else," I scowled back.

"I'm scared of going back Saara. Why are you even here? Aren't you scared of me?"

"I came here because dad's going mental thinking about you being back in town, why you're here, what you want, whether you're still that same idiot, whether he should turn up at your door, why you want to marry Faria - I mean come on, you've got *everyone* on edge Idrees!" I shouted out.

Shouting out was so not me, but I was just letting my emotions spill out. It was probably the first time I had shouted in a very, very long time. It felt weird. Normally I controlled my emotions and my anger really well, but right now I couldn't help it. For my parents' sake.

"You can't just turn up in the area ten years later, expect to marry Faria, expect for you to work secretly in the local hospital, and then *not* come and see your dad and family to say sorry to them! I mean who do you think you are? You're so senseless, and... and, *strange*, for thinking you don't need to say sorry after everything you did!"

Idrees was just staring at me from across the room, shocked.

"Well say something then!" I shouted pressing my hands down on the sofa.

"I err," he stuttered in his silence, "You're mature for your age, really. You are."

He carried on looking at me and then quietly said, "You remind me of dad."

I was touched at that comment.

"I do want to see dad. Well, I wanted to see all of you guys. But I've been worried at how you'd all react. I thought dad would go all crazy on me. The last thing I expected was for *you* to turn up at my doorstep."

"Well here I am," I said matter-of-factly. Maryam's influence was clearly rubbing off on me.

"Dad is aching to see you. You don't understand. You walking out of our house was probably the most sensible thing you did at the time..." I stopped, considering how insensitive my last comment must have sounded, but it was true.

I continued, "If you hadn't walked out, mum and dad were at the end of the road with you at that point, and they would have kicked you out themselves. So you saved yourself that embarrassment. Tell me one thing, have you changed?"

"I have, I promise you I have," he answered quickly.

"Well then what have you got to hide?" I stood up. "Turn up at our house tonight. You'll be doing another sensible thing, trust me. If you want to prove how much you've changed, you need to prove it to mum and dad, and, you need to apologise. They're your parents, they'll always love you. But you have to seek their forgiveness first."

I smiled at him. He looked upset, as if in deep thoght about what I had said, but he smiled back. I was glad, because it only proved to me that he genuinely cared and wanted to come back home.

"Thanks Saara, I..."

"Say thanks once everything's sorted." I smiled again.

I walked to the front door, and heard him shouting behind me, "What time shall I come!"

I grinned happily to myself - he was really going to come.

"Dad will be back home after six, let him eat etc, come at seven, I'll make sure we're all there," I answered.

I didn't wait for his reply. I opened the door and headed out, straight to Hannah. I smiled broadly when I saw her.

She stood up and grabbed my hand, squeezing it as we walked to the bus stop, not saying a word, knowing that I was happy with whatever had been discussed. *Alhamdulillah.*

CHAPTER 5

Time was going so slow.

It was 6.50 p.m., and I had been waiting for the clock to strike 7 p.m. for the last two hours.

I was fidgety and nervous, Saalihah knew what was going to happen, but my parents were completely unaware.

"Are you okay Saara?" My mum eyed me suspiciously.

"Jee mum, I'm fine!" I said, a little too high-pitched.

My parents knew me too well, they knew I wasn't acting myself. Just then the doorbell rang. I stopped squeezing the ball I was messing about with, and looked at my dad. He casually got up taking his reading glasses off, and walked to the door to open it.

There was silence.

"Idrees?"

"Dad..." said a quiet voice.

I heard my mum take in her breath. Her eyes were wide open and she quickly put down the book she was holding.

"Oh my... son... you've finally come!" I heard my dad exclaim.

There was a little ruffling noise and I could tell they had just hugged each other. My father was exclaiming and muttering to himself, most of which was shock and excitement at seeing his son after over ten years. *Such a long time,* I thought to myself. I was making silent prayers, that this meeting I had set up was all worth it.

My dad rushed into the sitting room, and looked at us all with wide eyes. He had tears in his eyes. I looked at my mum - she too had tears in her eyes, although I wondered whether hers were for happiness or fear of what Idrees was here for. Maybe it was both. I got up from the floor and sat next to my mum on the sofa, putting my right arm around her tightly.

She was as tense and stiff as a rock at the moment. Saalihah was curled up on the one-seater just watching everything unfold, amazed.

Ibrahim and Yahya were in the other room playing. Yahya popped his head round the door at the sound of doorbell, then disappeared into the room again, uninterested. He obviously didn't understand or remember the importance of the person who was in front of us right now.

"Ma..." Idrees said quietly looking at my mum. His face was flushed. He was so embarrassed - I could tell. All of a sudden my mum stood up and ran to him, hugging him and kissing his cheek.

"Oh Idrees!" she sobbed. "Where have you been hiding my boy!"

The pain and anguish in my mother's voice was evident, but what touched me the most was that this boy wasn't even hers. His mother had left him when he was young, but my mother had put everything to the side and tried raising him as her own, despite his abusiveness toward her and her 'own' children. But such was the love ingrained in my mums heart, based on the actions and practice of the Prophet Muhammad peace be upon him. Islam is truly beautiful.

I saw Idrees hugging my mum back tightly, his eyes closed.

"I'm sorry for everything," he whispered, and as he opened his eyes I was sure I saw tears in them too.

"Come and sit down," my mum said leading him to the third sofa in the room. "Make yourself at home please, are you hungry, have you eaten?"

"Yes mum, don't worry, please just sit down with me," Idrees looked up at dad as mum sat down next to him.

"Dad... I'm sorry to just turn up like this... I..." he looked at me. I just smiled, slightly shaking my head to hint at him not to mention me going to him.

"It's good to see you," I quickly said, to make sure he didn't have to fill the awkward silence.

"And you Saalihah," he smiled weakly at Saalihah, again, face flushing with embarrassment.

She was the eldest and would have remembered a lot more than me or the younger two.

She just nodded, and blinked a few times, still obviously fascinated at what was going on. I don't think she could believe that he'd actually turned up. She had been really sceptical when I told her I'd be going to see him.

"Why couldn't he think of coming himself? He obviously doesn't care about us Saara!" she had said.

"Sometimes people just need a push to do something good, maybe me visiting him will give him that push. He might have a million reasons for not having come to our house already," I had answered, in defence of him.

I remembered my manners and got up to get Idrees something to drink. I found some orange juice in the fridge and grabbed a few extra glasses - I assumed my parents would need something right now as well.

When I went back in, my dad was asking Idrees what he was doing with himself lately. I really wanted to know too, but I didn't want to get between their conversation.

'If things work out insha allah, I can ask him to fill me in on all those missing years later on,' I told myself.

"I was working in Manchester for a few years, and studying there too," I heard Idrees say.

"How did you manage to fund yourself? Were you working?" my dad asked.

"Yeah I had a part time job - nothing special - just at a local shop, but it paid the bills and gave me enough to save up... I was sharing my flat with a few friends so rent and everything else was pretty cheap."

"Why choose Manchester?" my dad looked at Idrees with piercing eyes as he said this.

Idrees stayed quiet for a moment. "I heard she was there, I thought I might see her." He looked down. "And she was. And I did see her. But some time later she was transferred down here again. I stayed on until my studies finished."

"Did she recognise you when you went to see her?"

"No," Idrees scowled. "She told the nurses she didn't want to see me."

"Why did you take Faria to see her then?"

Idrees didn't look up. "I thought she'd come round and be happy for me and talk to me if I went with someone like F..." Idrees trailed off, embarrassed.

My dad sighed and closed his eyes for a moment. My mum looked down.

"Idrees, she isn't going to come back. She isn't that woman you think she is. She needs to stay there so they can look after her, better than me or you can. She's in a better place!"

Idrees' face hardened, and he simply looked down.

My mum cleared her throat and handed a glass of juice that I had set on the table, to him. He took it and held it in his hands, but didn't drink it.

"I tried doing everything I could son, you know that don't you?" my dad said, his eyes still closed.

Idrees just nodded gingerly.

"And as upsetting as it was at the time, I'm glad that things worked out like that. Or I wouldn't have had this lovely family around me now. I wanted you to be a part of it, you kept rebelling, wanting nothing to do with us. You don't know how much everyone truly loves you, especially your Ma here. That's something *she* never did. Just let things go my son. I would never be saying this if I didn't truly mean it - she isn't going to get better."

They were talking about Idrees' mum, my dad's first wife, Husna. This was new territory for me, she had never been discussed in the house before. All I knew was that she had been extremely depressed and aggressive, and to protect himself and Idrees, my dad had to do something about her and they wanted to go their way separate ways. She then ran away, and my dad was glad of that. I assumed she was in an asylum, or a mental health clinic – I don't really know much about depression. I made a mental note to check it up on the Internet later on.

"So," my dad said clearing his throat. "You seem like a changed man Idrees. Have you left your past behind you, or does it still catch up to you?" He looked directly at Idrees.

Idrees took a nervous gulp of the juice. "I've changed dad, I promise."

"That's what I wanted to hear, *maasha Allah*. I hope you can *prove* it's true as well," my dad added, emphasising the last sentence.

"I swear, I just need a chance dad. I won't let you down... any of you. I just... I just want to make things right. I don't expect you to trust me or forgive me yet, but, I will try my best honest. I've never felt more alone in all these years. Living with lads, wasting time, no family, no nothing, I just... I can't explain how awful it is to be in that situation. That's why I tried to get out of it, to do something with my life. I know a nurse's job isn't the best but it was an easy opportunity for me at the time, I had a chance, so I went for it. Luck's been on my side."

He looked up at my dad, exploring his face for any sign of trust I suppose.

"There's no such thing as 'luck' Idrees, everything happens by the will of Allah, with His Permission, with His Plan," my dad said sternly. "Besides, there's nothing wrong with being a nurse." He paused. "What's this about you and Faria?".

Idrees fell into a nervous quietness again. "I... err... well," he began.

"You want to marry her?" my dad said.

"Yeah," Idrees answered quickly. "I do."

"I'm not going to ask you about how you got in touch with her, or for what reason you two began to talk. I don't want to know," my dad said, almost scowling. "Free-mixing and having a girlfriend or boyfriend, is haram. Clear cut haram. I don't want to know how much you love her, or whatever it is, because it's going to change my perception of you and her.

You're my son – you should be a man of respect, a man of honour. Having a girlfriend is not, and I repeat *not*, honourable. I want to trust you, and I want to help you, and I want you to have a good future, a good life, a good beginning to a new life. So from now on, I want you to deal with this girl, the way you ought to have dealt with her from the start.

If you're interested, I will approach her parents on your behalf. You will not, and should not contact her. Is that clear Idrees? You want my trust, then this is how it has to play out.

It is Islamically correct, it is the way we have been advised by the Prophet, and you have sisters yourself, who will one day marry *insha Allah*. I'm not having my son messing about with someone else's daughter, especially not my *friend's* daughter."

Wow my dad was so abrupt and honest. but it all made perfect sense, *alhamdulillah.* Idrees just nodded, and quickly finished off the rest of his juice.

"I won't contact her, I promise," he said as he put the glass down next to him.

"If they say no, then are you prepared to accept that also, Idrees?" my mum asked quietly.

Idrees looked quite upset as the possibility registered to him. He nodded though.

"However, we will try to make it happen *insha Allah.* I've already spoken to Aaliyah's dad, Abdullah. He speaks highly of you. He says you're very respectful, and caring. I hope you can show the same respect to my other friend who you owe a serious apology to."

Idrees nodded again, wringing his fingers.

"And by the way, if it doesn't work out, then don't worry Idrees, Allah has something better planned for you," said dad. "I need to know though, are you planning on sticking around for good, or are you planning on running out at the first problem you face?"

"Honestly dad, if you'll allow me to stay and see you guys, I promise you I'll stay. I really want to make up for the lost time. I hardly know my brothers and sisters. I'm the elder bro, I should be someone they look up to. And I really mean it, I'm really sorry for not coming to your house before," Idrees said nervously.

"It's not just *our* house Idrees, this is your house as well," my mum said quietly from the chair she was sitting on.

Did this mean Idrees would forever be in our lives now? I couldn't help but smile.

CHAPTER 6

"I'm off to Madrassah mum!" I said as I passed the kitchen.

"Okay Saara stay safe, see you soon *insha Allah*, assalaamu alaikum!" she shouted.

I was happy today. For a lot of reasons. Firstly, Saalihah had just passed her driving test and so I had planned a surprise for her. Secondly, Hannah had decided to start coming to Madrassah, and thirdly, Maryam's parents were going to give their answer to my dad today about Faria and Idrees, and whether they were happy with the marriage. I felt giddy about it, but I had hope in Allah that it would happen.

I wasn't sure what was said as my dad had gone over to their house alone a few days ago, but I was really hopeful and it seemed my dad was too when he had come home that night.

I walked past Hannah's house to pick her up and soon we were on our way. I filled her in on the basics of what I planned to do about Saalihah's surprise party. I had ordered a lilac Mini Cooper car cake and bought her a really nice hijab she had wanted from the sole Islamic shop we had in town. We were then going to call a few of her closest friends over, and my mum was going to cook some lovely food for us all. I was going to invite Faria too, but it would be weird if Idrees was in the house at the same time, so I didn't.

I asked Hannah to do du'aa as today was decision day for Idrees and Faria. Hannah was one of them girls whose du'aa always seemed to get accepted. She would wish for something, and it would just happen. Fascinating thought how Allah can answer your du'aa through somebody else.

Inside, I really wished they'd accept because if they didn't, I knew it would make things slightly awkward for us all, including me and Maryam, my dad and Maryam's dad, and the mum's as well. We were all friends.

Idrees had come to our house once more since that first day, but he was working long shifts and my dad told him he'd visit him tonight, after he'd spoken to Faria's parents.

"He must be so nervous!" said Hannah.

"I know, I can only imagine," I paused. "Even I'm nervous. You know Hannah, everything feels strange recently – in a good way. Like since the arrival of Idrees I mean, everything's suddenly become better."

"How's that strange? It's good isn't it," she asked.

"It is good. But it's strange because who would have thought, that a person who caused you so much pain can suddenly bring you so much happiness?"

"As always Saara, point well made," she smiled.

"It reminds me of sayings of Sahaabah and the Prophet peace be upon him himself. You know there's so much wisdom in what they would say. I bought a new book recently, and in it was a quote that said, "Don't love your friends too much, for they may become your enemy, and don't hate your enemy too much, because they may become your friend." I mean if my parents totally despised Idrees, they would never have noticed the change in him now, and would never have accepted him back. But they did, because inside they never really hated him. He was just a rebellious teenager. They got angry at him a lot yes, but he was always beloved to them. I'm just glad. That's all."

I breathed a sigh of relief as we reached the doors of the Madrassah. It was already open and we went inside. It was Hannah's first time coming today, she hadn't been to Madrassah when she was younger, and she was really apprehensive.

I touched her hand, "Don't worry Hannah, just be yourself, the kids are going to *love* having you," I smiled at her.

She smiled at me and we went inside. I started setting up the classroom benches, and Hannah got into action with me as soon as she walked in. She was so helpful in so many ways.

I taught the six-seven year olds how to recite. They were all on Qaaidah but because of the large class numbers, and the fact that parents had requested it, we decided to do classes on Sunday's as well, just for one hour. Because I was free and available, the Mosque had allowed it, and so the other sister from the Mosque and I would teach. Her name was Somayyah and her husband was the head-teacher. She was amazing, and had two twin boys who were in my Sunday class - Bilaal and Sa'd. They were exceptionally bright *maasha Allah*.

The hour was over in a flash and I was really glad that Hannah had enjoyed herself. I had wanted her and Maryam to come for so long, but I knew it wasn't their 'scene'. Hannah had never been to Madrassah and Maryam had only gone to one for a few years. In my view, it wasn't long enough, and so she had a very limited perception of how good Madrassah's can actually be. I totally loved ours, the teachers tried so hard and the set up and facilities were average, but the teachers made it the beautiful place it was, as did the students of course.

"Do you think I could start coming every Sunday, Saara?" Hannah asked as we began locking up.

"Yeah of course! I'd love it, and I'm sure Zaira would appreciate the help next week too!"

"Who's Zaira?" she asked whilst scratching some random paint off the wall.

"She's the third teacher, and she's lovely, I can't even begin to explain. She's heavily pregnant though and so struggles quite a bit now. She couldn't make it today but she said she would be in next week."

"Ha, heavily pregnant! After everything I've been through with my mum, I know how that must feel. I'll definitely turn up to help her," smiled Hannah genuinely.

"How's Aaliyah now?" I asked whilst tugging the door shut.

"Much better, thanks for asking. They keep calling her in for check ups but they're saying it's all looking good *maasha Allah*." She sounded so happy. "Oh, I forgot to tell you, I saw Idrees on Friday at the hospital."

I turned to look at her as we began walking. "Oh yeah?" I said.

She coughed. "Yeah... he looked quite worn out. Really upset type. I do feel sorry for him. My dad went up to him and they had a bit of a chat while we waited for Aaliyah's check up. My dad really likes him you know. Maryam's dad came down to our house last night.. I'm guessing it was to find out what my dad thinks of him."

"What did your dad say?" I said squeakily.

"Well... he said he's only ever known him as a decent guy. He didn't know about the past, so he was quite shocked. But he said from what he's seen of him now, he's a hard working and decent lad. Maryam's dad was really upset you know. I've never seen him like that before - so worn down and tired. I guess it's eating him up."

"Maryam said he's not spoken to Faria since that night," I said.

"Hmmm... I feel sorry for uncle. He's always been so good to everyone. I guess Faria is feeling really guilty right now, and so I feel sorry for her too. Everyone makes mistakes," Hannah shrugged.

"Yeah I agree... Did your dad say what his decision would be about the marriage thing?" I asked excited.

"No, he didn't. Or if he did, I wasn't there at the time. My parents and I had a good chat about it afterwards though. Mum was shocked too when she heard what had happened. They both dug at me for not having told them as soon as I found out from you and Maryam," she laughed. "I told them a secret is a secret!"

I laughed back, and then turned serious. "Hardly a secret now, half the college Faria goes to know what's happened! You know how it is, people love gossip, they can't keep their mouths closed," I said, angry that people would spread such stupid gossip about a girl. It was none of their business.

We reached Hannah's house. "Thanks for coming today Hani," I hugged her.

"No, thank *you* for taking me, I really enjoyed it, I really want to come every week now!" she hugged me back. "Come in Saara, I've got that USB stick you needed to borrow."

"Oh yeah thanks for remembering!" I followed Hannah in, took my shoes off in the hallway, and went into the living room.

"Idrees?

Chapter 7

Idrees was sitting comfortably on the sofa with Hannah's dad.

"How come you're here?" I asked confused.

"And a *wa 'alaykumussalam* to you too," he replied with a cheesy smile.

"Sorry, I forgot my manners. Assalamu 'alaikum to you all," I said embarrassed.

I kept forgetting that Idrees could obviously be at Hannah's house - he had got to know her father after all.

"Are you planning something secret together?" Hannah asked raising an eyebrow at her dad.

"Oh yes, no girls allowed in this business. Scoot!" said Hannah's dad cheerfully.

"I just came to pay the rent, and then thought I'd come in and see Aaliyah," said Idrees. *How thoughtful of him.* "I also came to officially invite uncle Abdullah to my wedding."

My jaw hit the ground as I looked at Idrees. He smiled back, super happy, super wide.

"No *way!*" shrieked Hannah from the kitchen.

"Yes way," replied Idrees, still with a smile plastered on his face.

I dragged my mouth shut. "That's such good news! I can't believe they've agreed!" I managed to say.

"Yeah *maasha Allah* - it is very good news. I'm glad that *alhamdulillah* it's working out as well. Idrees here is a good lad. He's got a long life ahead of him, and this is one of the first steps towards it *insha Allah*," said Hannah's dad smiling at Idrees.

"Thanks uncle, it means a lot to me - everything you've done for me. I mean, I hardly would have been in this position if it wasn't for you."

"For me? I haven't even done anything," said Hannah's dad confused.

"You did," said Idrees. "You gave me a decent place to stay in, you spoke positively about me to Faria's dad, you supported me throughout, you might not know it, but you did a whole lot. And I appreciate all of it."

"Well, let's just appreciate my baby girl Aaliyah instead of me then - because if she hadn't gotten ill, none of us would have met, and you wouldn't have that flat, and I wouldn't have said any good words about you to Sulaiman." He winked. "It goes to show, sometimes a problem happens in your life, and you think it's bad for you, when really, so much goodness comes out of it."

As he said this, he reached over and picked Aaliyah up from her cot. He lifted her in the air slightly and said, "This baby girl here, is the source of everyone's happiness in this room right now. Aren't you sweetheart?" He hugged her and she cooed in her baby voice. He was so sweet.

His words made me think though. It was true. Everything was a chain, and it began with Hannah's family, when Aaliyah was born.

When she got ill, and Hannah and her family were suffering in hospital, the reaction was starting - Idrees 'coincidentally' began working on Aaliyah's ward, he 'coincidentally' was chosen to be Aaliyah's nurse, he 'coincidentally' got chatting with Hannah's dad, and Hannah's dad 'coincidentally' had a property he could rent out to Idrees who 'coincidentally' was looking for a place to stay.

And it only sounded better if you went back a few years earlier, before Aaliyah was even born, when Idrees 'coincidentally' became a nurse, even though he originally wanted to be an IT technician - so he told me the other day.

'Coincidentally' Maryam had seen Faria and Idrees that day, and 'coincidentally' she had been in the garden when he threw the letter. 'Coincidentally' I stayed with Maryam and saw Idrees that day in the café properly, and Hannah who knew who he was - didn't.

'Coincidentally' Faria and Idrees disappeared that day, and 'coincidentally' Saalihah's friend's brother knew about it, and we all turned up and stayed in Maryam's house that night in order to see where they had both got to.

The list in my head carried on and on.

Except there's no such thing as 'coincidence' - is there?

Everything, and absolutely everything, happens for a reason. Allah alone knows the reasons why things in your life happen the way they do - but it's because of Allah that you should allow them to happen - and always say *alhamdulillah* - because the thing is, you really never know what's around the corner. The whole story might begin with sadness - but it'll most likely end in happiness. And if you don't be patient, and you don't remember Allah - you might never get that happiness, because you're too busy worrying or complaining.

Faria's family accepting Idrees was all the result of a chain reaction, and it was all because of Allah, in a way in which He had planned, and in a way in which He wanted. And it was simply beautiful.

I smiled and looked at Hannah just as Maryam burst through the doors with her father.

I looked at her with a huge grin on my face. *We had a wedding to plan.*

Final Comments

MARYAM

"Have you not packed your bags yet you dumbo?" I looked at her and sighed for the umpteenth time.

"Well if you'd just give me a minute Maryam, keep your hair on!" she shouted back.

Faria's suitcases were already packed since last night, but she decided she needed to 're-pack' them, 'in case' she missed something out.

"You know if you miss your flight tomorrow it'll be *so* funny..."

SAARA

Maryam's comment made me laugh - I couldn't help myself. Faria looked up and glared at her as she kept sifting through her things. Idrees came in with his suitcase and dragged it into the middle of the corridor.

"Mum, can this stay here for the night?"

"Don't leave it in the way Idrees, move it to the side at least!" mum shouted whilst looking out with annoyance from her bedroom.

Idrees looked around confused. "Which side?"

I sighed. "Oh you men don't know your geographic's very well do you!"

I huffed and dragged his suitcase where it belonged - *out* of everyone's way.

HANNAH

I smiled as I watched the panic the night before Faria and Idrees left for Hajj. It really was amazing how everything had worked out for both Saara and Maryam's families. Actually, me, Aaliyah, mum and dad were like a part of their family, and had been with them every step of the way on the wedding. It was a blast. *Alhamdulillah.*

Hey, it's not just fairy tales that have happy endings - Muslims have them all the time!

Park Royal Hospital
Swallow Road
Gillsborough

January 6th 2014

Mr and Mrs Yoosuf,

Aaliyah Yoosuf has been discharged from Royal Park Hospital care.

Please see the enclosed documents for the after-care plan. For any further concerns, please contact Dr Hussain's clinic.

Discharge nurse:

Idrees Ali

4pm tomorrow in Vicky's Café. you better be there...

PLS Furry.

Dear: Abdullah and family

You are cordially invited to the walimah of

Idrees Ali & Faria Naeem

Time: 5pm - 9pm

Date: Saturday 31st May 2014

Venue: Luxury Grounds Hotel

Hollyfield Gardens

Gillsborough

RSVP:

Zubair Ali & family

Sulaiman Naeem & family

And so, all three friends, Hannah, Maryam and Saara, continued to grow as Muslim teenagers living in their little town of Gillsborough.

They had become much stronger, much more patient, much more understanding of the world around them, and most importantly, much better Muslimahs who continued developing their relationship with Allah in every way they could.

Hannah wanted to become a children's doctor, to help other children like Aaliyah who were suffering from illnesses.

Maryam wanted to become a counsellor... but she decided she didn't have the patience, and settled to become an optician instead, because she felt she had a keen detective eye...

Saara continued teaching in the Masjid, and planned to fulfill her dream of becoming a doctor to travel around the world to help people. Idrees promised he would go with her. It seemed that helping people ran in their family!

All three girls began studying Islam on weekend classes in the Masjid along with Faria, who now, by the way, had completely turned her life around and connected to Allah.

And they all lived happily ever after...